TRAFFIC STOP

TRAFFIC STOP

FIRST EDITION

A Boner Book by
The Nazca Plains Corporation
Las Vegas, Nevada
2006

ISBN:1-887895-29-9

Published by,

The Nazca Plains Corporation ®
4640 Paradise Rd, Suite 141
Las Vegas NV 89109-8000

PUBLISHER'S NOTE
This is a work of fiction. Names, characters, places, and inci-
dents either are the products of the writer's imagination or are
used fictitiously, and any resemblance to actual persons, living
or dead, business establishments, events or locales is entirely
coincidental.

Editor, Blake Stephens
Cover Art by Ross Johnston
Art Direction, Robert Steele

For Mother Perry,
bless her heart!

TRAFFIC STOP

FIRST EDITION

A Novel by
Samuel Stephens
© Copyright 2006

Day One

I don't know where the hell I am.

Texas, sure, but beyond that I'm lost. I turned off I-20 over an hour ago, onto a state road I thought would take me to the job site, but that hasn't panned out. None of the landmarks are matching the map I got from the customer, and I've been trying to thread my way back to the interstate without much luck. It's a sure bet I'm going to be late, and I press down on the accelerator so at least I can get nowhere a little faster.

It's after 9 AM on a Thursday morning. The car smells of grease from the egg-and-cheese-McHeartStopper I had for breakfast, and the taste of bitter coffee is lingering at the back of my throat. This job site was the last stop on my road trip, and I was looking forward to heading home to Florida after this. For the hundredth time I berate myself for not having a cell phone - at least then I could call the customer and get directions. Well, there's bound to be a diner or gas stations around here some-where. I'll get directions there, make a phone call and be back on track before too long.

Outside my car windows Texas is mostly flat and mostly brown. The sun is coming up ahead of me, neatly tucked behind the rearview mirror, and I've got Marilyn Manson on the stereo to stave off fatigue. I didn't sleep well last night, and my eyelids are as heavy as bricks.

Police lights are going off in my rearview mirror, snapping me to attention. Fuck! I must have been dozing with my foot on the accelerator! There are two cops in the cruiser behind me, and since there's no one else on the road they definitely want me. I slow the car and pull over to the shoulder, kill the engine and the music as the cruiser pulls in behind me. The flashing lights turn-off. My heart is pounding in my chest. I've had speeding tickets before, but nothing more serious than that, and with my luck the gay and leather pride stickers on the back of my car just might buy me some extra shit from these two. They probably won't recognize the leather pride flag - most straights haven't caught onto that one yet - but the rainbow symbol is pretty well known. I exhale. This might be awkward.

The cops don't move for several moments, probably calling in my plate. They talk with each other for a bit more, drawing it out, before they open their doors. My stomach does a somersault. I roll down the window, then search the glove compartment for the registration. By the time I've got it and my license ready the troopers are flanking my car, one by my window and the other next to the passenger side.

"Good morning, Sir." It's the one by my window, the driver, speaking. I can't see much of him, because he's standing so close, but I get a good look at the thick, braided-leather duty belt around his waist. It's crammed with gear: flashlight, gun, ammo, nightstick, handcuffs, and despite my nerves, my cock wakes up in my pants. Police gear always gets me going, and there's nothing hotter that a good looking man in a cop uniform. It's not often I have the chance to admire one up close, and I don't know the Texas uniforms at all, so I let my eyes wander a bit and drink in every detail. His pants are dark gray with a blue stripe down each side, his shirt light gray, short-sleeves showing off thick biceps and forearms dusted with sandy-gray fur. I don't know if he's wearing boots, but I hope he is. I'll try to get a look in a bit. His hands are sheathed in tight, black leather police gloves, which are just too fucking hot for words, and I'm guessing he's over six feet tall.

"Sir," he says. He doesn't bother to lean down to look me in the eye, but I can see his name-tag: STEPHENS. "Do you know why we stopped you?" He's got a deep, rich voice, modest Texas drawl, full of self confidence and just a little edge to let me know who's in charge.

I can't help it: I imagine those gloved hands pushing me forward against the car, cuffing me, unlatching my belt buckle and dropping my pants by the roadside. . . My dick belches up some pre-cum. I shake my head and try to compose myself. "Yeah, officer, I was speeding. Sorry about that."

The cops glance at one another over the top of my car, and I take the opportunity to check out Stephens' partner. He's shorter, with a bit of a gut that suits him just fine. His forearms are thicker, tanned clay-brown and covered with black hair, and I see a tattoo coiling around his left bicep, peeking out from beneath his shirt sleeve. It might be a snake. He's wearing the same tight leather gloves. Oh man, my dick is raging hard by this point, and without thinking about it, I reach down and press my palm against my crotch. The pressure on my dick feels good, and I know I'm going to have to jerk off when I find that gas station or diner to make a call.

I hear a modest cough to my left. I look and see that Officer Stephens has stepped slightly away from my car, giving him just the right perspective to see me play with myself. I pull my hand away, probably too quickly.

"License and registration, Sir?"

"Right here, officer." I hand them over.

"I'll be just a moment." He turns and heads back to his cruiser. I watch him in the side mirror as he goes. He's got a beautiful bubble ass in those uniform pants -- which seem a little tighter than they really should be -- and his back is broad and strong-looking. Stephens is one cop who spends time in the gym and doesn't mind who knows it. He's wearing a Stetson the same color as his shirt, and I finally get a look at his feet. Damn, just boring black shoes. Oh, well, can't have everything.

His partner remains by my car, not bothering to walk around to my side, make small talk or acknowledge me in any way. They've probably figured out I'm gay, and probably don't think very much of the fact. I wait several minutes. There's the sound of crickets in the brush to either side of the road and no cars to break up the monotony. Wish I knew where the hell I was. At least I'll be able to get directions from these two when they're done giving me the ticket.

Finally Stephens emerges from his car again, plants the Stetson on his head and comes forward. He's wearing black aviator sunglasses, almost like he got out of bed this morning and decided: "I do believe I'll dress like some faggot's cop fantasy today." He stops at my window and plants his hands on his belt. "Sir, I'll need you to step out of the car, please."

I blink. "What?" I say quickly. "Is there some kind of problem?"

Officer Stephens turns fully toward my car now, puts both of those gloved hands on top the window slot and leans in. The Stetson shades his face and clean-shaven jaw. His sunglasses are impenetrable. He looks at me for several seconds before speaking. "I said: get out of the fucking car, *Sir*. Make me tell you again and you'll be even sorrier."

I think several things at once. First, that this isn't happening. Second, that they must have me confused with somebody else, a bank robber or a terrorist or something. Third, that this is incredibly, totally fucking hot! Receiving an order from Officer Stephens has made my dick so hard I think it's going to poke a hole right through my pants.

"Okay," I say, and quickly open the door. He gives me enough room to step out of the car and close the door behind me. By this time, his beefy partner has walked to this side of the car. He's also wearing sunglasses, and has a solid dark moustache. He's as woofy as his fucking partner, and I'm momentarily distracted.

Stephens lashes out and grabs my jaw with his gloved hand. Before I can react, he pushes me up against the car and kicks my feet apart until my legs are spread. I'm off-balance, leaning back against the car while he's bearing down on my chin. I make a quick, pleading glance at his partner, thinking he might put a stop to this, but that asshole is smiling like this is the best damn show he's seen all day.

Stephens leans in and puts his face to mine. I smell leather, coffee and aftershave, and I see my own wide eyes reflected in his sunglasses. "I got some fucking plans for you, asshole." He glares at me, like he expects some kind of reply. Without meaning to, I say two words. They are words practiced over years of submission to dominant Men, words filled both with desire and fear, words by which I live my life.

"Yes, Sir," I say.

He grabs me by the shoulder and spins me around, pushes me forward against the car and twists my arms backward. He cuffs my wrists with practiced efficiency. I just let this happen, try to be loose and not resist, figuring that's the best way to avoid getting hurt. I don't know what this means or how to react. They grab my upper arms and march me back toward the cruiser. Stephens' partner breaks off and opens the back seat, and suddenly, Stephens is pulling something stretchy down over my head. It's black and cool, and I realize as it covers my face that it's a nylon bondage hood. I've been in one of these before. All I can see now is a dim ghost-view of the world, framed with cross-hatched elastic fibers, and I feel a hand on my head, forcing me down into the back seat. They're none too gentle about it. I'm laying on my stomach, hands cuffed behind me, unable to see a thing. The car door slams shut.

Nothing happens for a few minutes. The sound of my breathing fills my ears, and the hood stinks, like somebody pissed in it. Then I hear the sound of my car engine starting, followed by tires on gravel. They're taking my car off the road. After a bit, one or both of them climb into the front seat of the cruiser and we start rolling. I hear Stephens get on the radio and tell a dispatcher that they're going off-duty. They don't talk. My heart is beating in my chest and my dick has finally gone soft. We keep driving. Ten minutes? Half hour? I have no idea. I realize only too late that I should be counting the number of turns we make, so I can reconstruct the path once I'm free. If I get free. It's hopeless anyway -- I was fucking lost to begin with! I do notice that the road gets rougher as we drive, until finally we must be on some rutted dirt lane.

Eventually the car stops. Stephens and possibly the other one get out, and I'm alone for several minutes. I listen hard, but all I can hear are more crickets and something rusted moving in the breeze. There's no traffic noise or even barking dogs. The car door at my head opens suddenly, and a shaft of sunlight falls across the vinyl seat in front of my eyes, sharp and painful even through the hood. The cops are two indistinct shapes. They reach in, grab me by the shoulders and pull me out of the car. I try to stand once they get me outside, but I trip and go down on one knee.

"Play along, fuck, or I swear we'll kick the living shit out of you right here!" It sounds like the second cop.

"Yes Sir!" I say quickly. "I'm trying, Sir!"

"Better fucking try harder," he says.

They pull me to my feet and I manage to stay there this time. They turn me and push me forward. I start walking. Through the hood I can see the outline of a building against the sky. It looks like a single story, a ranch I guess, and it seems to go on for a while. They tell me to stop as I approach the porch, then guide me up the steps and on inside. It's dark and cool in there and I can't see a damn thing. One of them takes the lead, clutches the front of my shirt and pulls me along. I can feel the soft glove leather against my chest. We march down two long corridors and into a room. They position me somewhere within and let go. I don't move. I hear a metallic -snik- behind me, and a moment later, something cold and sharp is laid against the back of my neck.

"Can you figure out what this is, fuckhole?" Officer Stephens asks.

"Yes, Sir. It's a utility knife, Sir."

"Good boy. Don't make any sudden movements or you might get hurt."

The other cop chuckles somewhere in front of me. "Yeah, wouldn't want that to happen."

Stephen's goes to work on my clothes. I feel his arms reach up my T-shirt from the back, and a moment later, the fabric is slit down to my waist. Two cuts more and the shirt is gone. One of them unlatches my belt and pulls it from my pants. They undo my shoe laces and order me to lift my feet. I comply, and before long, they've got me naked and cuffed there. My dick has gone semi-hard again, and I figure I probably got a long rope of pre-cum going all the way down to the floor. If so they don't mention it.

A hand on my back pushes me forward until my chest touches something rough. It feels like a wooden post. They unlock the cuffs but immediately bring my wrists together again on the other side of the post. They re-cuff me.

"Sit, asshole."

I sit. When I'm down on the floor with the wood at my groin, they tie my ankles with rope on the other side. They bring my cuffed hands down near the floor and tie the chain to some attachment point there. When they're done I sense them standing on either side, probably regarding their handiwork. It's still dark in the room, but I can see a fuzzy razor-line of sunlight leaking past a drawn shade. I'm breathing hard. It hits me like a thunderclap, just how fucking scared I am.

Then they leave. I hear footsteps cross the room, a door shut. After several moments car doors slam outside. The engine fires to life and there's the sound of tires driving away.

Fuck. Now I've got time to think. Could this be a kidnapping for ransom? I suppose so. All my personal info is in my car, and in my wallet, which I guess is still in my sliced-up pants. If they wanted to, they could try to get money for me. But something about that doesn't fit. Why had that first cop said he had plans for me? It was like he had been expecting me. They were both fucking hot: if they had wanted me to suck them off I would have gladly done that. My cock gets hard all over again, just thinking it. I'd show these two a good time if I only got the chance, and maybe that would keep them from hurting me. Or worse. That's something else to consider. Whatever their plans are, they can't intend to keep me here forever. I'm guessing they're real cops -- all that gear and the cruiser would be too hard to fake -- and even though I didn't get badge numbers or anything they've got to be easy for me to identify. So, logically, there's no way they ever plan to let me go. When they're done with me, I'm guessing the last item on the list is to put a bullet in my skull. That makes my dick go soft. I figure my only chance is to play along, cooperate, give them whatever they want and hope I see a chance to escape before they get tired of me. It's frustrating in a very strange way. These guys are my wet dream. I would gladly have paid for an experience like this, and here it is for free. I'm scared half out of my wits.

I assume I'm not being watched, so I feel around the post. It seems like a regular wooden fence post from the home center, rough-cut, four-by-four, attached to the floor with angle brackets. I try to jiggle it but no dice. I can't raise my hands by more than an inch or so, so I don't know how high it goes, but I imagine it's attached at the ceiling. If I lean down I should be able to grab the hood and pull it off my head. Yes, I. . . I stop. If I pull the hood off, I don't know if I'll be able to get it back on before they come back. Who knows how they'll react? I better leave it in place. Seeing the room probably won't help me all that much, anyway, and I don't guess I'm going anywhere too soon.

I don't know how long I wait. The room heats up as the day wears on. There's no air conditioning in this place, and by the way the temperature rises it feels like there's no roof insulation either. An old farmhouse? No, this is Texas, so it's got to be an abandoned ranch. I listen carefully but I can't hear any human sounds outside. I shout for several minutes but the only response is my voice bouncing back to me. Hours pass. My back hurts from the position they left me in, so I hug the post for relief. I wish they'd let me go to the bathroom. That coffee I had is ready to get out now. I hold it for as long as I can, but I have no idea when they're coming back. I finally just let it go. Warm, strong-smelling piss splashes across my stomach and chest. I've been sweating from the heat and fear, so it smells like I'm pissing orange juice concentrate. Afterward I sit in a puddle of my own piss and feel it go cold. I doze.

I snap awake when I hear a car engine outside. Did I dream that? No, there's a car door slamming. I don't know how long I was out. The room is very warm now: I can feel sweat trickling down my abs when I move. The inside of this hood still smells rank. Is that the same car? I hear the front door open and close, then some noises elsewhere in the ranch. Finally, after I'd gotten used to the sound of activity, the door to my room opens. I turn toward the noise reflexively, but I can't see anything. Two sets of footsteps walk toward me and stand on either side.

"Christ," one of them says. It sounds like the second cop from this morning. "Fucker pissed himself."

The other one, Stephens, sighs. "He'll just have to clean that, up I suppose. Isn't that right, fuckhole?"

I feel a shoe or boot tip nudge my naked thigh. "Yes, Sir."

"Damn right."

Some furniture is moved in the room, and one of the cops unties my ankles and unlocks my handcuffs. He pulls my hands behind my back and cuffs me again, then moves behind me, grabs me by the biceps and lifts me to my feet. I stand there.

"Stay," he commands.

I don't move. A moment later they turn me and march me to another part of the room. One of them leans in close to my ear. "Kneel, fucker."

I kneel. I've spent many hours on my knees, hands tied behind my back and naked before a Man. It's one of the positions in which I'm happiest.

I feel a hand bunch-up the hood fabric at the top of my head, then quickly remove it. At the same moment, a retractable window shade is lifted, flooding the room with sunlight. I blink furiously and turn away from the light. Slowly, my pupils adjust. One of the cops chuckles, and they both take seats on simple wooden chairs they've placed in front of me.

Yeah, it's my friends from this morning. They have both removed their Stetsons and sunglasses, and swapped their flat-soled black shoes for dusty cowboy boots. The other cop - FISCHER according to his name tag - has thick black hair going bald at the back. His build is meaty and a little soft, though he could take me down without a problem, handcuffs or no. He's definitely got some Italian in his background. Stephen's hair is silver-brown and cut short, his eyes the same color spiked with blue. He fixes me with a hard stare, softened just a bit by a confident smile.

"Having a good time, boy?"

There's no good answer here. Tell him "no" and I'm insulting his hospitality. Tell him "yes" and I'm obviously lying. I cast my eyes downward, keeping them trained on his boots, and decide on the second answer. I learned a long time ago never to lie to a Master.

"No, Sir," I say as meekly as possible.

He feigns surprise. "No? What's wrong, boy?"

Eyes still down. "I'm frightened, Sir."

"Hmmm. Well, I suppose I can understand that. Fear is a healthy emotion, boy, especially for someone in your situation. Hang onto that fear. *Obey* it, boy, and we'll get along just fine. Do you understand?"

"Yes, Sir."

"Good boy. I think we should have some introductions here. No need to be rude, after all. I'm Officer Stephens, and my partner here is Officer Fischer. When you address us, you will do so respectfully, using either 'Sir' -- which I see comes pretty naturally to you -- 'Officer Stephens' or 'Officer Fischer'. Repeat those names for me, boy."

I look at each of them in turn. "Officer Stephens. Officer Fischer."

"Good boy. Now, as for your name, I don't suppose that'll be a problem. For as long as you're with us, you'll be known as 'boy', 'fuckhole', 'asshole', 'dumbshit', 'fuckmeat', or anything along those lines. Can you understand that?"

"Yes, Sir. I am your fuckhole, Sir."

"Damn right," says Officer Fischer.

Stephens laughs. It's a genuine laugh, not unkind. "You're probably wondering why we picked you up. It's nothing scary, I promise. Here's the situation: Officer Fischer and I belong to a little. . . social club, you might say. We get together every so often -- just a gathering of friends -- and we got a meeting coming up this Sunday. The way our club works, though, is that every member has to bring along some help to run the party. Officer Fischer here, he's an associate member, so he's off the hook. But I need to bring someone. That's where you come in. I had a boy all lined up but he kinda. . . got loose, which left me in a real bad spot. When we stopped you for speeding this morning, though, you just seemed like a natural choice, so I decided to give you a shot."

I look up at them, suddenly hopeful. Can he be telling the truth? No, I decide, he can't. They'll never let me go. But my best chance lies in making them *think* I believe them. "Yes, Sir!" I say quickly. "I love to serve."

"You'll get your chance, boy. You'll get your chance."

Officer Fischer takes a cigar from his shirt pocket. He breaks the plastic wrapper, cuts the end of the cigar and then plants it in his teeth. He lights it up and starts blowing thick smoke toward the ceiling. I watch the lit end of the cigar glow and fade, glow and face, completely entranced. My cock gets hard all over again.

Officer Stephens glances at my dick and then at his partner. "Looks like someone's taken a shine to you, buddy!"

Fischer sticks the cigar in his teeth and crosses his arms. He stares at me. "Fuck I care."

Stephens shakes his head, as if disappointed. "Some folks got no manners." He claps his hands. "So! We've got a lot of work to do before Sunday. My partner and I need to train you to do what's expected, and we got to make sure you're in the right shape. Hell, considering all the work *we* got ahead of us, I half think it'd be easier to let you go and bring Fisch here as my fuckhole."

Fischer snorts and taps cigar ash on the floor.

"Well, maybe not. First thing I want to see, boy, is your boot technique." Officer Stephens extends his right foot and lifts the pants leg just a bit, exposing the worn leather of his cowboy boot. "You know how to show respect for a man's boot, don't you, boy?"

I nod. "Yes, Sir!"

"And how's that, boy?"

"With my tongue, Sir!"

"Damn right. Get down on your stomach and show me what you can do."

I wait just a moment to see if he intends to uncuff me first, but no dice. Very well: watching me struggle must be part of the program. I bend at the waist, shift my weight onto my right shoulder and ease myself onto the floor. This is nothing new to me. I wriggle forward until my nose is touching his boot, give one last glance up into those uncompromising eyes and get to work. I lick the boot leather with vigor, shoving my tongue into the space between the sole and toe, feeling the stitching in the crevice. His boot smells wonderful, a mixture of polish and fresh-cut grass, and when I glance up I see his gloved hand resting on his knee. God damn, I was made for this! I bring my tongue down the side and up over the arch of the foot, flexing my lower back muscles to gain some elevation. He shifts his foot just a bit to give me access to the other side, and I go to work there, saying "Thank you, Sir!" in the moments when I come up for air. My dick is raging hard now, and I rub it on the wood flooring as I wriggle back and forth, trying to get at every inch of his boot. I'm sure they enjoy watching my ass flex as I move about. Officer Stephens lifts the toe, revealing the underside, and I plant my tongue there without hesitation, licking the broad dusty plain of the sole. I taste grit between my teeth but I don't care. In a moment when I pause for air, I nuzzle my cheek tenderly against the underside.

Stephens presses his boot to the floor at that moment, trapping my cheek and face underneath. I wait and bear out the pain until he relents.

"Thank you, Sir!" I say.

"Work on the other boot now, boy."

"Yes, Sir!"

And so it goes. I inch myself over to his other foot and begin to clean the leather there, scraping my nipples and stiff cock on the rough wooden floor as I go. The officers are silent as I work, neither approving nor criticizing my performance. I see ash from Fischer's cigar hit the floor every so often, and the smell of his smoke cuts through the fatigue of my back muscles. When I've spent maybe five minutes on Officer Stephens' left foot, I am instructed to work on Officer Fischer's boots. I labor my way over there, wallowing in the dropped ash as I get to work and clean each of his boots in turn. My tongue gets dry and raspy. I can't taste much anymore, nor do as complete a job as on Stephens' boots, but I don't think they notice. Officer Fischer lifts his left foot and tells me to roll on my back. I obey, then wriggle closer to him until his heel is directly above my face.

"Open your mouth, fuckhole!" he says around the cigar.

I open my mouth, and he slowly brings the boot down, filling my mouth with the heel. I suck and slurp on it, flexing my stomach muscles and trying to get as much of the heel into my mouth as possible. I imagine myself sucking mother's milk out of the hard leather. My dick oozes pre-cum. I feel the slimy trace of it down my waist and onto the floor.

Officer Stephens stands up and towers over me. Fischer pulls his boot away and I watch it go, a bit sad. Stephens places his foot on my chest and presses down just enough to hurt. He smiles, so fucking sexy it makes me want to weep.

"Good boy," he says. "You keep up that enthusiasm and I believe everything will be okay."

"Yes, Sir!" I say, wincing through the pain. He removes his boot.

"Enough fucking around," he says. "We got work to do."

They uncuff me and help me to my feet. They lead me to a closet where I am given a bucket and scrub sponge. I am told to clean up my piss from earlier, which I do. In the process, I get a good look at the house. It doesn't appear to have been lived in for some time. In the rooms that I see, furniture has been removed or pushed into a corner. The room where they're keeping me was once probably a bedroom. There is no bed now, just three bondage posts attached floor to ceiling and several wooden chairs. My clothes are gone. I finish my task and return the items to the closet. I stand hands behind back, naked with eyes cast downward, and ask Officer Stephens if I might have some water from the tap.

"Oh, don't worry boy. You're about to get plenty of water."

I have no idea what he means by this but I keep my mouth shut just the same. They take me to a new room. I guess it had once been a bathroom, and the toilet and shower stall are still here, but the walls and floor are covered with plain white tile. There is a single floor drain in the middle of the room, several wall spigots and lengths of garden hose, and a stainless steel

IV stand on wheels holding two enema bags. Officer Fischer, his cigar now finished, orders me to stand against the far wall. He uses a garden hose to clean me off from head to toe. The water is cold and so forceful that it stings, but I take it without complaint.

"On your hands and knees," he says.

I get on my hands and knees. Water drips off my nose and lips. I watch it fall to the floor. The IV stand is wheeled toward me, and Fischer fills both bags from the garden hose. Stephens snaps on a pair or latex gloves and squats behind me. I feel his hands on my ass.

"Oh, fuck yeah!" he says. "We're gonna have some fun with this!" He squirts some lube onto my asshole and begins to finger me. I breathe deeply and try to open up my hole, but I'm cold and frightened and my ass has never been all that loose to begin with. "Tight little fuckhole here, Fisch. You may not be able to get that donkey dick of yours in."

"Oh, I'll get it in," Fischer says. I don't doubt him for a second.

Stephens slaps my ass with his open palm. "Fuck, yeah! It's time to clean you out, boy." I feel a plastic enema tip insert-ed, not roughly, into my ass. They begin to fill me with water.

I've given myself enemas plenty of times, but this is noth-ing like that. They fill me so full of water I think I can taste it at the back of my throat. I keep my head down and breathe deeply as the pressure builds in my gut. The water is cold, and I'm shiver-ing before long. The cops don't give a damn. They give me two bags, order me to lie on my side and lick their boots some, then get on my knees for more water. I go to the toilet and evacuate. Again and again we repeat the process. Their laughter echoes off the hard tile walls. Stand up, lie down, shit. Sometimes the water runs clean, only to turn messy again. Fischer uses the garden hose on me several more times to wash away shit dribbling down my leg. I become single-minded, focused on the goal of pleasing these men and emptying out my bowels.

I don't know how long it takes. Time is for other people, not for a fuckhole like me. These cops are patient, and they want me clean, so they keep at it. Finally they seem satisfied, but I am ordered on my hands and knees one last time. Officer Stephens smears more lube on my ass.

"Sometimes a hole like this can be unpredictable," he says. I feel something soft yet insistent being pressed against my anus. "Can't be too careful here, can we?"

It's a butt plug -- a big one by the feel of it. I bear down, trying to help ease it in. Officer Stephens rocks it from side to side and keeps pushing. *Christ* it feels big! But then, knowing my tight ass, it's probably nothing special.

"Open up for me, boy!" Stephens commands.

"Yes, Sir!" I grunt. "I'm trying, Sir!"

Finally he drives it home, and I give out a pained yelp. I'm breathing heavy, and I feel the rounded silicone base of the plug on my ass cheeks. My dick is hard again.

"You sure that fucker's in there?" Fischer asks. He's standing somewhere behind Officer Stephens.

"Hmmm. Don't know, Fisch. Why don't you perform some quality control?"

I look back just in time to see Fischer lift his boot and

drive the toe into the base of the butt plug. "Ungh!" The force translates up my body and rattles my teeth.

"Yeah, that ain't going anywhere," Fischer allows.

"Good."

They throw me a towel and tell me to dry off, then give me my sneakers and socks back. Once I've put them on they give me a jock strap and tell me to wear that. I obey.

They take me into another room, one that's been converted into a gym. Mirrors cover one wall. There are free weights, a squat rack, and some second-hand commercial exercise equipment. Soft rubber interlocking mats cover the floor. The gym is nothing fancy but it's well laid-out, and I bet this is where Fischer and Stephens work on their bodies. The room is warm, a single dented ceiling fan rotating listlessly overhead, and even though there are no windows I can feel afternoon heat radiating inward.

"So here's the situation, fuckhole," Stephens says. "Your sorry ass is going to be my contribution to the party on Sunday. I want you to look as good as possible. Now, there's only so much we can do in four days, but you're already in pretty good shape. The way I figure it, with our instruction, and the, uh, *special diet* we're gonna put you on, we should be able to bring out the cuts." He advances on me, stands in front with hands on hips. He looks down into my eyes, and I look longingly at his uniform, the badge and other glinting bits of metal. What would I give to be able to always stand like this, naked or nearly so before this Man. What would I give to always be his fuckhole? Quite a bit, I think.

He smiles. "It'll be just like having a couple of personal trainers, boy. Now isn't that what you always wanted?"

"Yes, Sir!"

"Then lets get started."

They put me through the most intense leg workout of my life. Squats are only the starting point. Lunges. Leg presses. They increase the poundage, order me to take more and more weight, grind out more and more reps. They bark orders, and I follow as best I can. Fischer chuckles when I collapse, tells his partner that they're finally getting somewhere. I've never worked this hard in my life. I've never been this motivated.

The room is hot, and sweat pours off my body. My jockstrap is sopping before long. Thankfully, they provide me with plenty of water to drink. Stephens and Fischer sweat too, stains spreading from their arm pits and necks as they order me from one exercise to the next. They don't let me rest for more than thirty seconds at a time, and all the while, I'm keenly aware of the silicone plug stuffed up my ass. It makes some of the exercises more difficult but I try to work around it, thankful that it's keeping me from making a mess, especially on the squats.

After a long while I collapse on Stephens' boots. "Please, Sir, no more! I can't take it! I can't do any more, Sir!" I look up, see him looking down at me.

For a while he says nothing. I'm afraid he's going to kick me. Finally, he exchanges a glance with Fischer, then looks down at me again. "Okay, boy," he says. "Kiss my boots, and we'll let you rest."

I thankfully kiss his boots, one after the other.

They take me back to the enema room. My legs are jelly so they let me crawl. They take back the jock, shoes and socks, and I am told to kneel at the center of the room, right above the floor drain. Fischer once again wields the hose to clean me off me. When he's done he sets the hose aside, stands with feet apart and arms crossed. "All right, fuckhole. Show me that ass."

I turn so that my ass is facing him. I brace myself for another kick to the butt plug, but instead, Fischer grasps the rounded base and pulls it free. I moan from pain and just a little pleasure as my sphincter is forced open again, slowly, and the mass is pulled from my rectum.

"Good boy. Go sit on the toilet."

I crawl to the toilet and sit down. There's some more shit to get rid of, but it feels mostly like water. Afterward, Fischer orders me onto the floor again and feeds another two bottles of water up my ass. By the time everything has been flushed away, Stephens appears in the room carrying a plastic drinking bottle. He sets it on the floor and looks at Fischer. "Is he clean?"

"As a whistle."

Stephens nods approvingly. "Good. You hungry, boy?"

I stare down at the floor drain. "Yes, Sir."

"Thought as much. Of course, we're gonna feed you over the next couple of days, but after going through all the trouble of cleaning you out we can't very well just put more food back in there, can we?"

I shake my head. "No, Sir."

"Damn right. So it's nothing but protein shakes for you until Sunday. Here." He picks up the drink bottle and brings it over to me. "Sit up, boy."

I do. The bottle contains a cup or so of dry whitish powder. My stomach rumbles at the idea of any amount of food,
even just the powder. It's been hours since I've eaten, and the
workout has made me ravenous. He offers me the bottle, but I
look at him, uncomprehending.

"Go ahead," he says, as if I'm too timid to drink.

"Hey, shit-for-brains," Fischer says to his partner.

"What?" Stephens looks back at him.

"You have to mix that stuff with water first."

Stephens slaps his forehead, his gesture exaggerated.
"Ah, hell, you're right. What was I *thinking?*

There are sixteen fucking spigots in this room but
Stephens doesn't go for any of them. Instead, he shakes his
head ruefully and unzips his fly, pulls out his cock. It's fat and
beautiful, cut but not terribly long, with a broad mushroom head.
He directs the cockhead down the spout of the drink bottle and,
after several seconds, starts a stream of piss going into the
bottle. "Ahhh. . ." He fills the drink bottle to near the top, returns
his cock to his pants and swirls the powder to mix it. What's left
in the bottle is a frothy mess the color of milky tea. He hands it to
me. The plastic is warm. It smells creamy and tart all at once.

My stomach flops. I've drunk piss before, but always from
a Man's cock, never mixed with anything. Somehow the idea is
revolting.

"You got a problem there, boy?" asks Fischer. There's
menace to his voice.

"No, Sir!" I say quickly. I put the drink bottle to my lips and begin to drain it. It's food, I think, and it won't hurt me. Thankfully I can't smell it, because I'm covering the bottle's spout with my mouth, but still it's got the greasy-sour taste of piss. The concoction reminds me of buttermilk, not only because of the creamy taste but also because Stephens used so much powder the consistency is about right. I finish it, honestly thankful that they gave me anything at all, and offer the bottle back to him.

"Good boy," he says. He fills the bottle once again with water from the hose and gives it back to me. "Here, wash that down."

"Thank you, Sir." I drain the bottle again.

"Now, boy. It's time for us to get some grub ourselves. But we gotta do something with you now, don't we?" He winks. "I got that all planned out."

Thankfully it doesn't involve the butt plug again. They put some padded leather restrains on my wrists and ankles and secure them with small padlocks. They also put a dog chain around my neck and lead me outside to the rear of the ranch. It's very difficult to walk, because my legs are so tired, but I try to hold it together. There's a yard out there, screened off with a fence and multiple trees. I see a picnic table and several vertical posts set in the ground. The sun is back behind the trees, long shadows stretching all the way to the building, and it's hot. They take me to the vertical posts and order me to spread my legs. I do. They chain the ankle restraints to the bottoms of the posts, my wrists to points about two feet above my head, leaving me in the classic "X" pose.

Afterward, the cops disappear into the ranch again for several minutes. When they emerge, they've got insulated food bags and bottled beer. They've removed their leather gloves. They sit at the picnic table not ten feet from me, open up the bags and have dinner. I see bar-b-que chicken and chips, condensation beading on the brown glass of the beer bottles. My stomach rumbles, and even though the air is still I imagine I can smell the food. They ignore me and talk shop, bullshit about co-workers, discuss the Rangers chances in the post season. They're definitely real cops -- either that or good actors -- and it sounds as if they both have wives. I stand tied to those posts and keep my mouth shut. My legs quiver from exhaustion. I shift position constantly, trying to find some way to get comfortable, but it's useless. Gnats fly around my head, buzzing my eyes and driving me crazy, but I can only shake my head from side to side to fend them off, like some kind of fucking barnyard animal.

Stephens and Fischer take their time having dinner. When they've finished and drained two beers apiece, there's a lull in the conversation. Fischer glances in my direction. "Guess we should take care of that."

Stephens follows his gaze. "Yeah, back to work, I suppose."

The sun has set now, and it's almost dark. They get up from the picnic table. Fischer collects the trash and takes it inside, and a moment later, outdoor lights strung along the building and fence come on. Stephens approaches me, no-nonsense look on his face again, like the meal and the beer primed his pump for something more. He stands in front of me for a few moments, hands on hips, and just stares. It's like he's evaluating me for the first time, and he's none too happy about what he sees. I try to stand at attention and keep my head up, focusing my gaze on some random spot just past his shoulder. He walks around behind me. I continue to stare forward, and eventually Fischer emerges from the ranch. Then I feel Stephen's hand on my right side, below the arm pit, just resting there. He runs his hands along my back, feeling the muscle beneath the skin. I've worked hard to keep my body fat low: when you're a boy hoping to attract Topmen, you've got to have something to offer besides an ass and a mouth. Stephens investigates the contours of my back, ass, and legs. I feel his hand on the crown of my head, firm and confident. He pushes my head forward and I drop my gaze.

Fischer joins him back there. I hear a plastic wrapper being opened, the hiss of a match drawn along the post to which I'm tied. Stephens walks around to my view, lit cigar stuck in his mouth. He puffs on it for a few moments saying nothing, just taking in the details of my body. I keep my attention on the glowing red coal at the end of the cigar. Please, I think, don't burn me with that.

I feel Fischer's hands on me now, palms running along my waist as if frisking me. He moves down, caressing my legs, then up, probing my armpits and arms. God, the feel of his rough hands against my skin is wonderful! My cock is hard again, long strand of pre-cum reaching down to the dusty ground. Stephens puts the cigar back in his mouth, crosses his arms and gives a small nod.

Suddenly Officer Fischer slaps my ass hard. I tense up but keep silent: the surprise is enough to cut off any yelp from me. His swat is followed by another, and another, and another, all landing on my right ass cheek. I grit my teeth and pull against the restraints. Fischer moves onto my left cheek, then my right, back again, swatting harder each time. I wriggle, trying to get out of the way even though I know it's hopeless. Finally I cry out. "Please stop, Sir!"

Stephens is all over me then. He leans close until his face is mere inches from mine, the business end of the cigar nearly singeing my moustache. I shrink back as far as I can, but I don't gain more than an inch of space. "You got a fuckin' problem, boy?" he asks around the cigar.

I give my head a tiny shake from side to side. "No, Sir."

"If you ain't got a problem, then why ain't you thanking the good officer back there for his attention, boy?"

"I'm sorry, Sir!" I say quickly. "Thank you, Sir!" I shout over my shoulder.

Fischer simply grunts and lands another whack on my ass.

"Thank you, Sir!"

Fischer likes beating a boy's ass. He works me over for a while, spanking my ass, my thighs, swatting the back of my head. Sometimes he reaches around from behind, firmly seizes my torso with his arm and just wails on my ass. He lands ten, twenty whacks on the same spot, measured increments of time between each, relentless. His bicep is thick and hard beneath the cloth of his uniform. The badge on his shirt front bites into my back. I cry out at the top of my lungs, trying desperately to remember to say "thank you, Sir" between the yelps. Officer Stephens stands before me and watches. He smokes his cigar and enjoys the show.

The action stops a moment, and I hang there slack against the restraints. I look down, see drops of sweat fall from my face to join the puddle of pre-cum I've left on the ground. That's when I feel Officer Fischer's boot against my fleshy buttocks, driving deep into the muscle, and I know I've got more coming.

I float away at that point. I'm shouting and I'm feeling the bite of Fischer's boot against my ass but it's almost happening to someone else. I'm surfing the endorphins. I become aware that Officer Stephens - tall and broad and strong and so fucking beautiful in his cop uniform that it makes me want to cry - that Officer Stephens has his own raging hard-on. It's tenting up his dark gray pants, modest blot of pre-cum darkening the fabric, and I want. I *want* to be Officer Stephens' boy, want to give him everything he could possibly desire, want to be held in his gaze for the rest of my life. Is he feeling it too? Can he read my mind? It seems about as plausible as anything else that's happened today.

Stephens steps forward then, pushes my head back gently until he fills my vision. He stares at me a few moments, cigar clenched in his teeth, searching my eyes. "Fuck," he says finally, so quietly that only I can hear, so tenderly that I will never doubt his words. "Fuck."

"Thank you, Sir," I whisper.

"You got more comin', boy. You know that, don't you?"

I nod. Only small movements are necessary in this place. "I know that, Sir."

He nods himself, as if we have just agreed to something. In fact, we have. He turns to look over my shoulder at Officer Fischer. "I'm about ready to nail this fucker to the wall, Fisch. How about you?"

"I thought you'd never ask."

"Fuck yeah!" He regards me again. "You like to suck cock, boy?"

"Yes, Sir!"

"You like to have your asshole raped by big cop cock, boy?"

I close my eyes, picturing that. My dick jumps. "Oh, yes Sir!"

"Well, good. You're gonna show me how bad you want that, fuckhole!" He steps back a few paces and removes the police baton from his belt. He lifts the hard wooden end and presses it to my upper lip, just beneath my nose, where it collects the sweat that's beaded there. "Smell it, fuckhole." I close my eyes and inhale deeply. It smells incredible, leather and smoke and power.

"Suck on it, boy. Show me how bad you want that cop dick!"

He pushes the end of the baton into my mouth, and I close my lips around it. I suck. I suck as if it were the stiffest cock in the world. I imagine it black and shiny, irresistible. I tongue the spot where a piss hole would be. I open my mouth wider to try to take its entire length. Stephens drives it deeper until it's pressing the back of my throat, until it will go no further and I gag. I shut my eyes tighter and concentrate. His baton is the axis of the world. I revolve around it.

"Suck it, fuckmeat," Fischer says in my ear. "Suck the fucking paint right off that damn thing."

I suck harder, straining to move my mouth up and down the wooden shaft. I'm moving my entire body now, back and forth, swaying, consumed with the baton as much as I consume it. I open my eyes and see Stephens smiling, cigar clenched in his teeth. He takes the baton out of my mouth, returns it to his belt, and spits out what's left of his cigar. Then he closes in on me, grabs the back of my head and covers my mouth with his.

He kisses me deep and forcefully, driving his tongue into my mouth, claiming me. I taste smoke and beer and it's enough to make me drunk. I push my pelvis against his, try to give my hard cock some relief against his uniform. Fischer envelops me from behind, reaches out, grabs my restrained forearms and presses himself toward Stephens, trapping me in the middle. It's as if I'm the sail of an ancient ship, and Officer Fischer is the mast. I'm crushed between the cops, helpless, restrained.

And I have never felt so happy.

Stephens finishes his kiss and backs away, chest heaving. He looks past me at his partner. "Let's take this fucker down. I'm gonna bury my cock up that pretty ass!"

"You ain't the only one."

Stephens frees my ankles, and Fischer undoes my wrists. He pins my arms behind me and reconnects them there, whispers in my ear: "Walk, fucker!"

I walk.

They march me back into the house, to a different room this time. This one's got a bed in it, a home-made affair with a simple frame made of rough lumber. There are no sheets or pillows on the bed, just a mattress. The room's also got more wooden chairs and a couple of cast-off nightstands topped with lamps. Stephens points at the floor before the bed. Kneel, fucker."

I kneel.

They stand beside one another in front of me, so that my face is at crotch level. I gaze up to look into Stephens' eyes. He's got a half-smile on his face as he unzips his pants and pulls out that fat cock. He holds it out to my face. "Go to work, boy."

I shut my eyes and wrap my mouth around his cock. I have to open wide, and even then it's impossible for me to keep my teeth completely away from his skin. The dick is soft to begin with but it hardens by the second, and soon it fills my mouth. I work at sucking him off. He grabs the back of my head and rams his dick further down my throat. For all its width it doesn't gag me, and I have no trouble breathing while his pubic hair fills my nostrils. The smell of his crotch makes my dick jump, and I lean forward to bury my face deeper. Back and forth, back and forth, I work on his cock. I wish they would release my hands, so I could use them as well, but instead I have to settle for rocking my head from side to side to give an extra dimension to the blow job.

I feel another hand on my forehead, Fischer, and he pushes my skull back until Stephen's cock falls out of my mouth. Fischer's got his own dick out now, long and dark and already hard, and I turn to swallow it. He's a bit easier to suck, since my tongue has room to maneuver. I outline his cock head and explore the piss slit. His crotch smells wonderful, musky and ripe, and I feel like I could stay here the rest of my life! I open my eyes enough to see him standing over me, uniform shirt open now, big pecs perched above a modest beer belly, everything covered with thick dark fur. Stephens is reaching over, pinching Fischer's nipple, and Fischer leans backward and moans. I suck and suck until finally Stephens grabs hold of my head and forces his own dick back into my mouth, displacing his partner's.

We keep at it. My knees ache from kneeling, and I'm losing feeling in my hands, but I don't complain. I time my breathing to mesh with the strokes on their cocks, inhaling on the outstroke, exhaling on the instroke, accommodating them in every way I can. They're greedy with my mouth. Sucking Officer Stephens. Sucking Officer Fischer. Back and forth. When I've got one in my mouth, I can feel the other's dick resting against my cheek, poking me in the eye, demanding, warm and wet from my spit. I can tell them apart by the flavor of their pre-cum. I imagine I can taste what they had for breakfast.

Stephens has got his shirt open now, chest hard and defined with no beer belly to conceal his sixpack, everything dusted with short gray fur. I like to look up at him while I suck him off. He returns the gaze, confident and in control. Stephens smiles down at me and pulls his dick out of my mouth. "All right, fucker. Stand up."

I stand up. Officer Stephens closes his mouth over mine and kisses me strong and deep. He fucking *owns* my mouth. Fischer unties my hands and I bring them around Stephens' waist, rub away the numbness. Stephens ends the kiss and pushes me back a step. Fischer man-handles me over to the bed, pushes me down face-first so that my legs are on the floor and my ass is up in the air.

"Don't move asshole," he commands.

Stephens is on the other side of the bed. He opens up the nightstand drawer and tosses something in front of me - a polyurethane condom. "Open that, fuckhole,"

I begin opening the package, stunned. These two abduct me, brutalize me is so many ways, and yet when it comes to fucking they're gonna use condoms? I don't understand, but I don't guess that matters much.

Stephens tosses a jar to Fischer standing behind me. A moment later I feel Fischer's hand on my ass, fingers prying apart the cheeks to expose my hole. A dollop of something warm and greasy is smeared there. It feels like petroleum jelly, which would explain the polyurethane condom. Fischer works the lube into my sphincter with first one, then two, then three fingers, opening my hole like a pro. In front of me, Stephens removes his police belt and lays it across a chair back. He's unarmed now, and I'm not tied up, but I don't dare try anything funny. Besides, I don't want to avoid what's coming next. Stephens undoes the top snap of his pants, and I can see everything now, continuous line of fur from his pecs all the way down to his fat cock. God-fucking- *damn* he's gorgeous! He struts around to the other side of the bed where Fischer has just finished lubing up my ass. I feel my legs pushed apart, and I can hear from the sound of his boots that he's standing between them now.

After a moment, Fischer walks into my field of vision. He's produced a cigar from his pocket and he sticks it in his mouth, lights it. I watch him puff to get it started, mesmerized, and at that very moment I'm surprised by the pressure of Stephen's cock against my asshole. Oh, Christ, it feels too big! It's almost like he's trying to jam a lemon in there! I grit my teeth and bear down on my ass, opening myself up as best I can. I've never been a talented bottom. Stephens forges ahead, slowly but insistently driving his cock into my asshole. I shut my eyes tight, reach back and grab my cheeks to spread myself wider. He's past my first sphincter now, and even though it hurts like fuck-ing hell, I don't ever want him to stop. I hear his voice, quietly repeating: "Uh-huh. That's right, fuckhole. Open yourself up for me. C'mon, boy. Gimme what's mine. . ."

With one final push Stephens forces himself home. I cry out from the pain and the shock. Then I relax, just a bit, because I know that's the worst of it. He stays there a moment, contracting then relaxing against me, getting my asshole used to his cock. Then he pulls out and comes back home, rocking his hips, and the fun begins. Stephens sets up a rhythm like a waltz. *Ba-ba-bum. Ba-ba-bum.* In and out. Back and forth. I breathe deep and melt into it. He's got me wide open now, com-manding my hole. Thankfully he's not slamming into the back of my rectum, which always hurts. No, this feels good, so much like dancing I almost hear music. I obey his rhythm as we rock on the bed, and he's talking quietly, mostly to himself, saying: "Yeah, take it boy. That's a good little fuckhole. Take my big cop cock. Yeah, boy. . ." I want to encourage him, to cheer him on, but I know that the rules here are different. I'm nothing but a piece of meat to these two, and they probably want their meat to keep quiet. I settle for trying my best to make my body accommodate his cock. It's the best fuck I've ever had.

While this is going on Officer Fischer watches. He's got the cigar going good now, and he's blowing smoke into a thick cloud that hangs around him like a blanket. Slowly he peels off his shirt, stands there bare-chested. I can see the tattoo around his left bicep clearly now. It *is* a snake, a rattler by the looks of it, and while the tail rests just a few inches above the elbow, the length of it coils up onto his shoulder before crossing over to his left pec. The mouth is wide open, fangs bared and about to clamp down on the nipple. Fischer's body glistens with sweat in the lamplight, the image softened by the smoke, and his dick is still out. He strokes it from time to time while he watches. I'd love to slurp on that piece of meat again but that doesn't seem to be in the cards. I belong to Officer Stephens at the moment. He's fucking me harder now, driving his dick into my ass as deep as it will go, grunting with each stroke. He's got his fists planted beneath my armpits. The mattress squeaks with each thrust. I wish I could play with my cock, rock hard and trapped beneath me, but I know better.

Finally Stephens' grunts turn to groans and increase in pitch. He fucks me harder and harder, faster and faster, saying "Fuck you. Fuck you. Fuck you!" over and over again.

"Yes, Sir," I say very softly. "Thank you for fucking me, Sir. Thank you for giving me your huge cock, Sir."

I don't think he can hear me above the bed springs. Wham! Wham! I'm like a tunnel now, nothing but a hole, my cock throbbing as he nails me to the bed. His groans build into a final guttural shout, loud and frightening, and he holds his dick in there and just spews. I think I can feel it pumping. I bend my legs backward at the knee as he relaxes, collapsing his weight against my ass. I hear him breathing ragged and fast, feel his sweat drip onto my back.

"Fuck. . ." he says between breaths. "Fuck. . ."

I close my eyes and exhale. Fuck is right.

Officer Stephens rolls off me then, onto his back beside me on the mattress. I look over and see his chest heave, cop badge rising and falling, short hair slicked with sweat. He's incredible. I want to thank him, reach out and gently touch his nipple, stroke the fur on his belly. I start to lift my hand.

It's Officer Fischer who stops me. "On your back, fuck-hole."

I look up, alarmed see him standing there across the bed. I'd forgotten about him. His arms are crossed and the cigar is clenched in his teeth. His dick is hard, leaky and throbbing with his pulse. "Yes, Sir," I say quickly, and roll onto my back so that my ass is suspended off the side of the bed. Officer Stephens gets up languidly and snaps his pants closed. Officer Fischer walks into view. "Legs up," he commands.

I lift my legs, presenting my freshly-fucked hole.

Fischer doesn't remove his police belt. Instead he retrieves the jar of lube off the floor and smears some of it on his dick. He taps ash onto the floor before putting the cigar back between his teeth, grabs my ankles and prepares to fuck me.

"Uh-uh," Stephens says. He's now behind me. Fischer looks up, catches something Stephens throws at him. It's another condom package. "Put that on," Stephen says.

"Mother fucker. . ." Fischer swears, softly. He tries to tear the package open but his hands are too slippery. He tosses it on my chest. "Open that, fuckhole."

I tear open the package with my teeth and remove the condom. Officer Fischer thrusts his dick forward, still rock hard, and I cover it. Then he leans back, lifts my ankles slightly and plows in without pause. I cry out. His cock is narrower than Stephens' but he drives it all the way in, punishing the back of my rectum. Fischer chuckles around the cigar, watching my face twist with pain.

And he fucks me. He fucks me hard. Fischer isn't content to pick one angle and go for it. He likes to explore. He repositions himself, first this side, then that side, looking for the routes that cause the most pain. He laughs when my eyes screw tight. I realize that the more I react the worse he makes it, so I try to make my face wood. This ruins some of the fun for him, so he settles in for a normal fuck. He is one hot cop, there's no denying that, and when my ass numbs up I even begin to enjoy it. As with Stephens, I'd like to reach up and touch his nipple or rub his belly, enhance the experience for him, but I think it's best if I just lie here and take it. My ass is doing a remarkable job. If I weren't a prisoner of these two I would never be able to take a fuck this hard. They've got me properly motivated.

Fischer builds himself to a climax, and while I'm watching, he starts grunting and his thrusts become erratic, looking more like seizures. "Fuck, yeah!" he shouts, and very quickly, he's there. He exhales, sending a long stream of smoke overhead, eyes shut. He rests his pelvis against my ass, and chest heaving hard, drops the cigar to the floor. He looks at me, leans over and pounds my chest with a closed fist hard enough to hurt.

"Fuck, yeah!" he says.

"Nice piece of ass, huh?" Stephens asks.

"It was probably better before you made it all sloppy."

"Quit whining. You'll get first crack tomorrow."

Tomorrow. Jesus Christ, tomorrow. My dick is hard but getting softer. I wish they'd let me jerk-off, this is the hottest scene I've ever had in my life -- but I don't dare touch myself without permission. I've served Top men before and learned that lesson well.

Stephens looks at me. "Stay, fuckhole."

"Yes, Sir."

The cops get dressed and clean up the room. I notice it's pitch black outside the windows. I have no idea what time it is, but it's difficult to care. I'm disconnecting. They told me they would keep me until Sunday. It might as well be next year.

Fischer disappears from the room and comes back with several lengths of rope. "Spread eagle on the bed, boy."

"Yes, Sir." I stretch out on the bed.

Stephens puts the wrist restraints back on me and they tie me to the bed posts. They give me enough slack to move a bit, but not enough to try to untie myself or jerk-off. After they're done, Stephens turns out the lamps and leans over me. He slaps my belly several times, open palm, each smack harder than the last. He smiles watching me tense up.

"Time for you to get some rest, boy. You've got a long day ahead of you tomorrow."

I look up at him, pleading with my eyes. Please let me go, I think. I won't tell. Just please let me go.

"Come on," Fischer says. He's standing by the door, silhouetted in the light from the hall. "I've got shit to do yet."

"All right," Stephens says. He looks at me for a moment, gazes up and down my body. And in the moment before he turns and walks to the door, he winks.

I stare after him in amazement. Even as he pats Fischer on the back, and they shut the door behind them, I'm still staring.

Had he done that? Had he winked at me? Or had I only imagined it?

If he had, what did it mean? Anything? Everything?

I don't know. I don't have time to wonder about it, because now it's time for sleep to come and command my body, just the way Stephens and Fischer have done all day.

And it does.

Day Two

I'm awake sometime later. I don't know how long I've been out - thirty minutes? Three hours? No way to tell. I stare into a corner of the dark room and listen to the crickets outside. I don't want to believe my memory of the previous day, but when I shift position on the mattress I find restraints holding me down. It's real. All of it's real. I tug on the restraints. If I work hard, enough I can just barely touch my nose with a finger but that's it. I'm not uncomfortable, but I'm not going anywhere either.

I've got a raging hard on. I can feel it now, the head of my dick resting against the fur just above my pubes. That's what woke me up. If I thrust my pelvis I can slide the head of my dick against my belly, just a tiny bit. Is it enough to jerk off? I try, thrusting several times. The mattress springs creak beneath me and the sensation just makes me harder, raising my dick head up and away from my belly. I'm stranded. Damn! All I can think of is Stephens nailing my ass with that beautiful cock of his. My ass feels sloppy but it itches like it wants more. I whimper. I'm alone and horny and I want to jerk off but I'm tied to this bed and I can't do a damn thing!

I go slack and relax into the ropes. I breathe hard for several moments.

I wish it were a dream.

I'm glad it's real.

I wake sometime after dawn. My mouth is dry and I thank

God I don't need to pee. The drawn window shade is luminous, struck by the sun outside and casting the room in a dull amber glow. I get a better look at the place. There are a couple of mis-matched chairs, two beat-up nightstands topped with thrift store lamps. There's a pattern on the wallpaper but it's faded from time, peeling in the corner where the roof seems to leak.

Someone is moving inside the house. I hear the clink of china, water running, the sound of boots on floor boards and male voices. Fischer and Stephens. Whatever they're doing they don't seem rushed about it. I lay there and wait. I'm starting to drift off to sleep again when suddenly I'm aware of someone in the hallway outside. A moment later the door opens and Fischer enters. He's wearing a black T-shirt, sleeves rolled up to show off his thick arms, snake tattoo visible on the bicep. The shirt fabric is taut across his chest, and there's an emblem on the left pec, something official-looking. He's got black military pants on, lace-up combat boots and a pair of black aviator sunglasses.

He approaches the bed. He's carrying another plastic drink bottle one-quarter filled with powder, and he looks down at me for several seconds. The emblem on his shirt is legible now, a round Texas shield with the words "POLICE ATHLETICS" inscribed within. Damn, he's such a hot fucker! I don't want my dick to get hard but I don't see how I can stop it.

"Got your breakfast here, fuckhole."

"Yes, Sir," I say. "Thank you, Sir." And I mean it. Even though I know what he's got planned I don't care. My stomach rumbles at the thought of food. Fischer chuckles humorlessly and sets the bottle down on the nightstand. He unzips his pants and pulls out his dark cock, points it down the mouth of the bottle. After a moment's effort he gets a good stream of piss going -- dark, strong-smelling morning piss. He must have been saving it for me. He fills the bottle, caps and shakes it to mix the powder. "Lift yourself up, boy."

I lift myself as far up off the bed as the ropes will allow, straining with my abs. Fischer supports my head from behind and raises the bottle to my lips. I catch a quick scent of it -- burnt coffee and butter -- and then drink the ochre mess down as quickly as I can. My tongue is so dry I barely taste it. I lick my lips when I'm done, trying to get the last little bit that's dribbled down my chin.

"Good boy," Fischer says. "Maybe you'll work out after all." He sets the bottle down and stares at me. "You still hungry, boy?"

Of course I am. "Yes, Sir!"

"Well, I got a nice fat piece of breakfast sausage for you here." He reaches down and strokes his cock. It's uncut and semi-hard, the head just beginning to stand proud of the fore-skin. I have to admit it does look like sausage. "You want a meal, boy?"

I know the correct answer to that one. "Yes, Sir!"

Fischer climbs onto the bed and straddles my chest. The metal eyelets of his boots are cold and sharp against my ribs, and his cock, stiffening by the moment, fills my vision. There's a drop of piss at the end there, golden in the morning sunlight. It falls onto my tongue as I open my mouth wide. I taste it this time, sour and strong, but just a split second later Fisher is grabbing the back of my head and forcing the whole thing down my throat. I gag, not prepared. He chuckles again.

"That's it, fuckhole. Enjoy your breakfast."

I relax my throat, concentrate on giving myself to him. I

work on the bulk of his dick with my tongue. He's got my skull with both hands now, raping my face the way he did my ass last night. I strain at the ropes, try to shift to get more comfortable, gagging. "Yeah, fuckhole," he moans. "You got some gravy where that came from."

Difficult to breathe. I try to inhale around his thrusts but he keeps throwing off the pattern, intentionally making me gag. I concentrate, wrapping my lips around the shaft, aware of his weight and the rope around my wrists. His moans get lower and more frequent. It feels like he's about to let go, and not a moment too soon. I'm feeling light-headed from lack of air.

"What the fuck is going on here?"

Fischer stops suddenly at the sound of Stephens' voice behind him. I open my eyes but I can't see beyond Fischer's belt buckle and the T-shirt stretched across his belly.

"I was just giving the boy his breakfast," Fisher says.

"Yeah, I can see that. Quit fucking around, Fischer. We got work to do this morning. Burt's going to be here before long."

"Yeah, well, I'd be finished by now if you hadn't walked in."

Stephens approaches the bed, into my field of vision. He looks down at me. He's dressed the same as Fischer though he's not wearing sunglasses. I have this fucked-up desire to wish him a good morning, but my mouth is still stuffed with Fischer's cock. Stephens pats Fischer's shoulder. "You're finished now, bud. Remember, he's *my* piece of ass, not yours."

"Shit!" Fisher pushes my head away and drops one leg

off the bed. He plants the other foot on my chest and pushes himself up. The rubber boot tread is rough and sharp against my bare skin but I don't cry out.

"Put that thing away," Stephens says, gesturing toward his cock. "Man, I can't leave you alone for a second."

Fischer stuffs his meat back into his pants, zips up and gives me a nasty glare. I look quickly after Stephens, pleading with my eyes, but he's already leaving.

"Let's get him cleaned up," Stephens says over his shoulder.

He may as well have said 'cleaned out'. Fischer unties me and orders me up. I nearly collapse the moment I stand, my legs sore as hell from the yesterday's workout, but Fischer steadies me. He takes me to the tiled room where I am once again instructed to get on all fours. The enema equipment is set up, and he flushes me out until I run as clean as one of the wall taps. It doesn't take nearly as long as it did yesterday. Afterward I'm given the butt plug and a small jar of lube and told to plug myself up, which I do without complaint. My ass is still loose from last night's pounding. I towel off and am allowed to put on socks, sneakers and a jock. Through it all Fischer watches impassively. He hands me an unopened liter of orange juice. "Drink that. You're going to need the energy."

I do as I am told. The taste of the juice nearly makes my mouth explode, and I notice for the first time that my head is throbbing from caffeine withdrawal. I don't suppose these bastards are going to offer up a double-tall latte next.

Fischer manhandles me over to the gym, where Stephens is waiting. He has me stand at attention before him, feet apart, hands clasped behind my back. I keep my eyes slightly downward as he circles me, inspecting me. My dick stiffens inside the jock. Stephens comes around to the front again, considers, reaches out and wordlessly takes my right nipple between his thumb and forefinger. He squeezes hard. I wince at the pain but keep silent. Finally he relents. "Breathe, boy," he commands. "No sense in you passing out."

I breathe deeply.

"We're going to start with push-ups, but believe me, we ain't gonna stop there."

And we don't. Stephens punishes me with the most intense chest and tricep workout of my life. The push-ups are easy -- enjoyable, even, as he orders me to kiss his boot at the bottom of each rep -- but from there we move on to bench presses. I normally work out alone, and I stay light on the bench because I'm afraid I'll get stuck mid-movement and look foolish, but that isn't an issue here. Stephens' coaching gives me confidence and his commands supply the motivation. It isn't long before I'm leaving puddles of sweat on every surface I touch.

I'm grinding out tricep press-downs. Stephens stands behind me with a leather paddle, and when my muscles fail before the end of the set he gives my ass one whack, hard, for each missed rep. I imagine the paddle frothing my sweat into a fine mist. Damn it hurts! I channel the pain into the workout and time ceases. There is only the weight, my fatigue, and Stephens' voice guiding me through it.

Eventually there's the sound of a motorcycle outside. Fischer? I haven't seen him for a while. But no, it sounds like a bike arriving rather than pulling away. Hadn't they said they were expecting someone? Stephens doesn't react to the sound but simply orders me to complete the set. I'm moving slower and slower, and by now even the paddle can't force more reps out of me. He seems to realize I've got nothing left, and snaps his fingers. "All right. Kneel there, boy, facing the door."

I hobble to the spot indicated and kneel. Long trails of sweat drip down my pecs to the dusty rubber matting. My chest seems huge, much bigger than it did an hour ago when the work-out started. I know that's impossible, but still, even the mirror tells me I'm different. Kneeling here on the floor, abused, hungry and nearly naked, I feel flushed with accomplishment.

Stephens stands behind me. He places his knee between my shoulders and helps me through some pec stretches. He stops just short of snapping me like a wishbone but damn it feels good! Afterward he pushes me forward. I lie face down on the floor, grateful for the rest, and he plants his boot on my buttock and applies just enough pressure to let me know he's there.

"You done good, boy. You done good."

I close my eyes and savor the sound of his voice, the feel of his boot tread on my ass.

There are other voices within the house. I recognize Fischer but he's talking to someone else. There's a third voice as well, younger and deferential, but I don't hear that one much. I can't make out what they're saying over the sound of my heart-beat. The voices come closer down the hallway, accompanied by the tramp of boots. The room feels incredibly hot, as if my ears are on fire.

Fischer enters the room. I look up just enough to see his boots. "You done in here, bud?"

"Yeah. Fuckhole's pretty much wrung out by now. He's a hard worker, though, at least when properly motivated." I hear Stephens slap the paddle against his palm.

"Yeah, I bet," Fisher says. "He's here." Fischer takes several steps into the room and then moves aside to let someone else enter.

I see the boots first: harness style motorcycle boots coated with grime from the road. Tucked into these are tight denim jeans -- old and well worn -- a leather belt and western-style leather vest. He's shirtless below the vest, well-defined sixpack and pecs sweat-slicked and accented with black fur. He wears a leather armband above his left bicep and clutches a leash in that hand. Eventually I lift my eyes to his face. He is handsome with blunt features, trim moustache and short black hair. He looks down at me with confidence. Instantly I recognize that this man is accustomed to seeing bare-assed men lying on the floor and staring up at him.

"Good to see you, Burt," Stephens says. He steps toward the man and they embrace. The place on my ass where Stephens' boot had been feels cold without it.

"I see you're busy," Burt says. "Up to your old tricks?" He's got a Boston 'southie' accent, sexy as hell.

"Yeah, just finishing up. Gotta get the little fucker ready for Sunday. You sure you can't stay?"

"Sorry, no chance. Got plans for the boy further west." Burt jabs his thumb back over his shoulder. I remember the leash in his hand and trace it back to a figure standing in the shadows behind him. There's a pair of feet there in short black boots, naked beefy calves with black hair.

"Ah, well," Stephens says. "Duty always calls. In fact, we gotta get him cleaned up here. Get yourself a beer and we'll be along."

Fisher and Stephens take me back to the enema room. They hand me a bar of soap -- the abrasive kind meant for removing grease -- and hose me down. The soap hurts against my nipples and ass but it's nothing compared to what I've already endured. They collect the butt plug and give me a towel to dry off, then let me put the sneakers back on. Stephens shoves a large silicone gag into my mouth and cinches it tight.

I am taken deeper into the house to a room with a pool table. There's a modest bar with booze and mixers, a refrigerator, pine paneling on the walls and an elevated shoeshine chair in the corner. Burt is sitting in the chair, enjoying a cigar while his boy licks the dust from his boots. The boy is taller than me and beefy in a natural, diffident way. He looks to be in his late twenties, his legs and chest hairy but his pubes trimmed to highlight his cock. His face is clean-shaven and handsome. I could easily be a top for a guy like this, though given the circumstances that's unlikely. The boy is naked except for the boots and a stitched leather dog collar around his neck. His master still holds the leash. The boy is completely absorbed in licking his master's boots and doesn't even look up when we enter.

"How about a game, buddy?" Fischer asks Burt.

Burt blows smoke toward the ceiling. "In a little bit. Want to get these clean first."

Stephens looks at me. "You know how to shine boots, fuckhole?"

I nod. I do well enough.

"Well, Bobby here is a fucking genius with the shoe leather, aren't you, boy?"

"Sir! Thank you, Sir!" The boy says quickly, barely removing his tongue from his master's boot.

"Hey, Burt," Stephens says. "You mind having your boy show the fuckhole here how to properly shine a boot? I can always use a good bootblack."

Master Burt taps ash from the cigar. "It'd be my pleasure."

I expect Stephens to remove the gag from my mouth, so I can lick the boot as well, but this doesn't happen. Instead he retrieves shoeshine equipment from a cabinet -- polish, cloths, daubers, tissue paper, brushes and the like. He hands these to Bobby, who motions me closer. I obey.

"First thing you want to do is give them a good buffing," he says. His accent is more New York than Boston, his voice slight in contrast to his frame. He takes one of the cloths and begins drying his own spit from the handsome boots. "Like this." He hands me the cloth. I take it and follow suit. Stephens pats me on the back while Fischer racks up a game of pool. Master Burt watches impassively.

So begins my instruction in bootblacking. We spend what seems like thirty minutes laboring over Master Burt's Chippewas. Bobby teaches me patiently, careful and precise in his direction. This is clearly something he enjoys. I suspect he could have finished the job by himself in ten minutes but he takes the time to bring me along. "Not like that" he says softly, wraps his hands tenderly around mine. "Like this." Several times I forget that I am gagged and try to thank him. Bobby doesn't laugh at me. Our work is occasionally interrupted by calls from the cops to get them beers from the refrigerator. Master Burt finishes and stubs out his cigar. When we're done, finally, the boots nearly show a reflection.

"Good boy," Master Burt tells Bobby. He pats the back of Bobby's head and Bobby nuzzles his cheek against his master's leg with genuine gratitude. Burt stands up and goes to a wall cabinet. He comes back with a gag which he inserts into Bobby's mouth and ties tight. It's not a plug like mine but a piss gag, a round tube now positioned within Bobby's open mouth.

"On your knees, boy," Master Burt says. Bobby immediately obliges. Burt stands before him and unbuckles his belt, unsnaps his fly and pulls out his cock. He holds the head just outside the tube leading into Bobby's mouth, and several seconds pass before he works up a good stream of piss. Bobby gulps it all down, never taking his eyes off his master's face. My cock goes stiff. Stephens and Fischer are taking in this show as well.

"Uhhhhhh. . ." Master Burt groans as he empties his bladder. Afterward, Stephens settles himself into the shoeshine chair. He holds me with his gaze and points at his right boot. "Okay, boy, let's see what you've learned."

I shine Stephens' boots while Fischer and Master Burt play pool. Bobby looks on and serves drinks as necessary, eventually taking a load of piss from Fischer as well. I'm glad they didn't fit me with the piss gag but I'm also just a little jealous of the attention being paid to Bobby. I work on the boots, rub the leather hard to melt the wax just the way Bobby taught me. I end up producing the best shine of my life. Stephens approves of my work, and Fischer seats himself for a shine.

By the time I'm done working on Fischer's boots the men have gotten tired of pool. Master Burt approaches me. "Stand up, boy. Turn around and give me a look at that ass of yours."

I do as I am told. His rough, callused hand firmly takes

hold of my ass, and he drives a meaty finger into my crack. I brace myself against the wall to keep from toppling over.

"This is a nice piece of ass you picked up here, Bud."

"Thanks," Stephens says. "He don't know shit yet but we're working on that."

"I expect you are." Master Burt opens my hole with a finger. I'm still loose and lubed up from the buttplug a little while back. "You mind if I take the little fucker for a test drive later?"

Stephens considers. "I suppose that could be arranged."

"Yeah," Master Burt mutters. "I'm gonna bury my meat up there."

I notice Bobby staring at me. His expression is stoic but with a hint of jealousy.

Afterward we are taken to another room. It's the one where I was left upon first being brought to the ranch, empty save for some chairs and three wooden posts fastened floor and ceiling. Bobby and I are positioned against the same post, facing one another with the post between us. Stephens ties my wrists around the small of Bobby's back, leaving enough rope so that I'm not stretched uncomfortably. Bobby's Master does the same to him so that we are tied to one another in a loose embrace, the rough four-by wooden post between us. Our ankles are tied together and I am fitted with a bondage collar which is then latched to an eyelet screwed into the post. Bobby's neck is chained in a similar fashion. When they're done the men stand back to admire their handiwork.

"I don't suppose they'll get into any trouble like that," says Master Burt.

"Well, you never know with boys now, do you?" says Stephens. "You two be good while we're gone. No playing! You understand?"

We both nod, and with that they leave the room, shutting the door behind them.

I stare straight ahead into the grain of the post, waiting. They could come back at any second and I don't want to get caught trying to communicate with Bobby. I haven't got much room to move but it's not uncomfortable. If history is any guide we could be left here for several hours. I count my breaths, close my eyes and lean my forehead against the post. This is the first chance I've had to collect my thoughts all day.

Bobby doesn't appear to be a captive. He seems to be Master Burt's boy of his own free will -- either that, or Burt has broken his will. Regardless, he most likely doesn't understand I'm being held prisoner, even if his master does. He may be able to help me get free if I can just get the situation across to him. This gag is going to make that difficult, though.

I decide to wait a bit more. My hands are tied in such a way that my palms are positioned above his muscular butt. I cup his ass and give a gentle, amicable squeeze. Bobby returns the favor and my cock responds by lifting itself against the splintered wood of the post. Bobby's got hair in the small of his back but stubble across his ass cheeks. Burt must shave him there. My fingertips rest against his crack and I begin to probe him, kneading and massaging and getting closer to his hole.

"Uh-uh," Bobby grunts forcefully through the hole in his gag. I stop. Fingering him must be a privilege reserved for his

Master. The last thing I want to do is upset Bobby. As a conso-
lation, Bobby begins massaging my own ass. It feels nice but I
can't let myself give into the sensation.

I tilt my head so that I'm peering past the edge of the post.
"Mmmmph! Mmmmph!"

Bobby tilts his head to look at me as well. His eyes are
placid, but he raises his eyebrows slightly.

"Elll eeeee!" I try to say "HELP ME" around the gag but
it's unintelligible. I shake my head and furrow my brow, try some
more. Bobby just looks puzzled and removes his hands from my
ass. He must think I don't want him to touch me. I can see his
tongue through the round tube of the gag.

I shake my head forcefully. "Mmmph! Mmmhphmmph!"
It's no use. Since Bobby can't very well separate himself from
me he simply rests his hands against my back. I give up, shut
my eyes and rest my head against the post.

Hours pass. Bobby is a damn hot boy and under any
other circumstances I'd love to be tied to him like this. Hell,
even under these circumstances my dick decides to enjoy the
situation anyway, and starts oozing pre-cum. Before long a wet
slick strand of it reaches all the way down to my foot. Through
mutual agreement, slowly and silently negotiated over the next
hour, we begin to explore both each others bodies and the limits
of our bonds. When Bobby shifts himself just so I can reach the
muscles of his upper back. This I do and massage him there.
I find his skin scarred in long furrows -- has he been whipped?
Bobby's arms are longer than mine. We discover that he can
reach the very tops of my hamstrings, just below my buttocks,
and he massages my sore muscles. The pleasure is enough to
make me collapse helplessly against the wooden post. Bobby
is tireless and affectionate, content to comfort me while not

demanding the same in return. Master Burt has trained him well.

Does this violate Stephens' warning about not playing? I don't know but it's hard to care. We shift position, working in concert to figure out which parts of our bodies are accessible. We embrace tighter and tighter until the rough wood of the post bites into my chest -- erotic and enjoyable on its own. Our caressing and massaging builds in intensity until we're both moaning through our gags. But finally, through fatigue or mental clarity we realize that further effort in this direction will result in an incriminating mess and probably splinters. We exhale and relax against the ropes, the post, and each others bodies. The resinous smell of the wood is strong in my nose, and I've come to associate it with Bobby's beautiful physique, learned more through touch than sight.

We wait. There are footsteps elsewhere in the ranch, the sound of boots on floorboards and muffled voices. The front door closes and the ranch is silent for a long while. I think they've left us. I don't even bother trying to attract Bobby's attention. I couldn't get the point across last time and besides, I think he's sleeping. I'll have to wait for another chance.

The sound of boots outside the room wakes me up. My hands have gone numb resting against the warm curve of Bobby's ass. Bobby is awake, looking toward the door behind me. It opens on squeaky hinges. Footsteps approach. Something is set on the floor, and Bobby watches the visitor come closer. I feel a hand press firmly against my ass. It's gloved -- I can tell that much -- and meaty. I guess it's Fischer. The visitor doesn't speak and I don't turn my head to identify him. The hand slides up my back, over Bobby's tied wrists, to my neck. It smacks me across the back of the head. The visitor leans in close, brings his mouth next to my ear, a bushy moustache tickling the lobe. It's Fischer.

"Yeah, fucker," he croons softly into my ear. "You got a problem there?"

I shake my head.

"No? Looks to me like you got a problem," he says. "Looks to me like you're tied up good 'n tight, some nasty fucker lookin' to rape that pretty boy asshole of yours. I'd say that's a problem."

"Emmmph phurrr," I say.

Fischer wraps his arm around my neck. He chokes me, forcing my chin upward and my torso away from the post. Bobby presses himself against the post to give me extra slack but still the ropes bite into my wrists. Fischer covers my ear with his mouth. "I'm fixin' to breed you, boy," he growls. "I'm gonna fill you up with my cum until it's leakin' outta yer goddamn ears. I'll get you away from Stephens before this is all over, and when that happens, your ass is mine. You understand, boy?"

I don't make a sound. It's too difficult to breathe.

Fischer tugs harder until my vertebrae are about to snap. "I asked you a fuckin' question, boy!"

I make a sound then, something between a whimper and an affirmative *Yes SIR!* Fischer must hear it because he lets me go. I collapse against the post, hugging myself to Bobby on the other side and breathing deeply. Fischer swats my ass hard with his open hand.

"Mmmmphphph!"

"Just a taste, fuckhole. Just a taste of what you got comin'."

Fischer unties Bobby, reties my ankles to the post and my hands behind my back. He leads Bobby from the room. I probe the knots of my ropes. Fischer did a hasty job of retying me and I figure if I work at it for a while I could get free. But what if I only get the job halfway done before he returns? I stand there like a good submissive fuckhole for maybe ten minutes. Fischer comes back. Wordlessly he removes my gag, unties my neck and ankles. He turns me around and instructs me to kneel before him. I do. Fisher is still wearing the T-shirt and military pants, the sunglasses and the leather gloves. He towers over me, and looking up into that impassive face I think I could happily stay here forever in the thrall of these men.

"Time for dinner, boy."

There's another drink bottle on the floor, already filled with white liquid. Fischer retrieves it and raises it to my lips. I open my mouth and begin to drink. It doesn't taste like it's been mixed with piss but I may just be getting used to it. I finish the bottle.

Fischer takes me outside to the back yard where I'm surprised to see that it's already dusk. Master Burt and Bobby are off in a corner of the yard. Master Burt has removed his vest and stands there bare-chested, while Bobby has been untied and freed from the gag. His master is giving him some quiet instruction, to which Bobby listens attentively. The back yard lights come on, and a moment later Stephens emerges from the house.

"Untie him," he says to Fischer. "They've got work to do."

Fischer drops his sunglasses to the picnic table and unties my hands. I watch as Master Burt finishes his instruction. Bobby nods in understanding, and his Master gives him a quick kiss. They turn and head toward us. Bobby looks so content it makes me want to cry.

We are told to make and serve dinner to the men. We set places for three on the picnic table with plates and utensils from the house, get them beers. Someone has gone to the super-market for bagged salad, pre-made pizza shells and toppings. I almost laugh when I see this: I like to cook *and* get fucked, so on some level this is shaping up to be the perfect weekend. Bobby has more experience at domestic service so he takes charge, makes sure the men are satisfied while I prepare the pizzas. We serve them and stand nearby while they eat, Bobby behind Master Burt and I behind Officer Stephens. I am grateful for Bobby. He gives me a template, an example of a good boy, and if I can just follow his lead maybe I can get out of this alive. Success could hinge on convincing Stephens and Fischer that I'm really enjoying myself and won't turn them in if they let me go. Hell, I *am* enjoying myself -- my dick says that often enough. If I could only be sure that they wouldn't hurt me, but then, the fear these men create has been instrumental in pushing me beyond my normal limits.

They drain their beers one after another, and not only do we fetch more for them but we also serve as their urinals. Beer-piss is just a shade stronger than water so this isn't bad. I dis-cover I don't mind in the least drinking from Stephens' beautiful fat cock. The evening wears on. The men talk of other people in their circle of friends. It's clear that they know a network of Masters, many of whom will be arriving at the ranch on Sunday. Master Burt regrets that he won't be here for it. Stephens and Fisher talk about the police department. I gather that homosexu-ality -- or at least homosexual acts -- are more common than I would have guessed or ever hoped for, and that many straight cops have figured out they can make extra money catering to the fantasies of gay bottoms. File that one away in case I ever get free.

Fischer asks Burt why he doesn't keep Bobby shaved all over, and Burt answers that he prefers to fuck men and not twinks. Of course, he keeps Bobby's ass shaved and crotch trimmed because he likes that effect. Stephens looks at me and considers.

They finish their meal. Bobby and I clear away the dishes. I stay in the kitchen to clean up while Bobby attends to them outside. Through the kitchen window I watch Bobby light their cigars. I finish and present myself outside just as the last of the cigars is stubbed out. Stars are shining and the conversation is winding down.

"Well, men," Stephens says, glancing from Fischer to Master Burt. "I do believe we've got some recreation."

Master Burt casts his gaze at me. "Damn right."

"Shoot, you should have been here last night," Fischer says, pointing at me. "He was tighter before we opened him up."

"Ah, well," says Master Burt. "Fuck 'em enough times and you wear 'em out, eh?"

Stephens reaches around and swats my ass. I jump. "This one's still got some use in him, though. Just you see."

They stand. Stephens attaches a chain to the collar around my neck and leads me back into the house. Master Burt does the same to Bobby and they follow along behind, Fischer bringing up the rear. We are led into the bedroom where I slept last night.

"Turn on those lamps, boy," Stephens commands. I do and return to him. He removes the chain from my collar and tosses it to the bed table. He spends a few moments looking into my eyes and I return his gaze, feeling strangely proud and capable. Follow Bobby's lead, I tell myself. You're Officer Stephens' boy. Act the part. The others have entered the room. Master Burt disconnects the leash from Bobby's collar and pushes him down on the bed. Stephens manhandles me into a corner of the room and turns me to face the wall. My hands are grasped from behind and tied tightly with rope. The gag is placed in front of my face and I obediently open my mouth to accept it. I can't tell what's happening over on the bed though from the sound of the bed springs it's pretty active. I am turned toward the door but still can't quite see what Master Burt's doing to Bobby.

Fischer is behind me. He captures my neck in the crook of his arm and holds me there while Stephens kicks my legs out to either side, forcing me to lean backward. Stephens makes a show of pulling on his gloves, places his hands on my chest. Fischer's meaty arm blocks my view but I can feel Stephens' hands roam across my body, stop to pay attention to the nipples. He starts to work them, rubbing my nips through the leather loves, ramping up the intensity until he's clenching and pinching them. Back and forth, one side to the other, he tugs mercilessly on my tits while Fischer voices encouragement. My nips are on fire. I whimper around the gag and struggle but Fisher just tightens his grip on my neck.

Over on the bed I hear Bobby moan.

Stephens leans close and stares at me, power and lust in his eyes. He holds up his left hand and removes the glove. A moment later I feel it slap across my abs. Whack! He leans in again until his face is inches from mine, nods silently. Whack!

Whack! Two more across my belly, harder.

"Here we go, boy," Stephens says.

Slap! Whack! Back and forth Stephens whips my stomach with the leather glove, each blow coming harder and faster than the last. It stings like hell and though I try to endure without complaint it doesn't take long before I'm overcome. I struggle against Fischer and get nothing for my trouble but a sore windpipe. Stephens moves the glove up to my nipples and whips them. I scream into the gag. No one's ever made my nips hurt this bad -- it's like he's stabbing them! The struggle makes me light-headed.

"I'm ready over here," Master Burt says.

Stephens lands one last whack across my chest and I scream in response. After a moment Fischer slowly relaxes his grip. I stand unsteadily, leaning forward with fatigue, ass brushing against the snaps of Fischer's pants and the rock-hard bulge beneath the fabric. They turn me toward the bed. Bobby has been tied to it in a 'Y' pose, legs fastened together at the bottom center, arms apart and tied to the top corners. He is gagged as well, his dick hard and pointing toward his chin like a compass needle. He turns to look at me, helpless and beautiful. Master Burt stands on the opposite side of the bed, massaging the bulge in his jeans.

"I'm going to enjoy this show," Fischer says in my ear. Stephens walks me toward the side of the bed, removes my sneakers. "Get yourself on there, fuckhole, and straddle that boy's cock."

He supports me while I climb onto the bed. I trudge on my knees until I'm straddling Bobby's legs, shimmy my way up until I'm positioned more or less above his cock. If they intend for me to fuck myself, with both of us tied like this, it's going to be pretty awkward.

Master Burt is at my side. "Bend forward at the waist, boy. I got you."

I do as I am told, Master Burt lowering me until Bobby and I are gag to gag. My weight is taken by my knees on the bed and my chest against Bobby's chest. My nipples scream at the pressure while Bobby's beautiful eyes fill my vision. Hands grasp the collar around my neck, rotate it, and with a metallic snap the D-rings on each of our collars are fastened together. Now we're restrained neck to neck, my ass in the air, my hands tied behind my back.

"Damn fine work, Burt" Stephens says. There's the chime and flash of a digital camera going off in the room. I don't want to crush Bobby but there's not much I can do about it. Thank God he's beefier than me. I exhale when he inhales, inhale when he exhales. Our breathing drifts in and out of step. When we inhale together the collar connection pulls taut like a boat lashed to a dock at high tide. Something cold and flat is lain across my lower back. "There you go," Fischer says. "Why don't you warm that ass up first?"

Burt takes the object. It's definitely a paddle. "Don't mind if I do."

The paddle is held against my ass cheeks for a few seconds. I close my eyes and relax my neck. The paddle is cool but it won't feel that way for long. Bobby grunts softly, a small sound of intimacy. The paddle is taken away from my ass.

I'm suddenly aware that my dick is as hard a granite, laying alongside Bobby's.

WHACK!

The paddle bites into my ass. I scream into the gag and try to wriggle away, but the restraints hold me fast.

"That was one, boy," Master Burt says.

"Emmmph, phurrr!" I shout into the gag.

WHACK

Master Burt nails me again on the same spot -- the bony part of my ass just above the hole. I whimper. Bobby hums warmly just inches away.

"That's two, fuckhole."

"Emmmph. Phurrr."

WHACK! He moves on to the fleshy parts of my ass. WHACK! He nails me again. Each time the paddle lands there's a flash across my vision. I don't know if it's the digital camera or just my imagination. I'm breathing hard now, almost snatching the breath from Bobby's nose. Sweat lubricates the skin between our chests. Down by our crotches I can feel a slicker pool of pre-cum. Bobby arches his chest to support me, lifts his head to nuzzle my cheek and temple.

WHACK! Flash. Each time the paddle lands it takes me one rung down the evolutionary ladder, until finally I'm just a mindless thing wriggling in a warm slick den. Master Burt's counting means nothing to me. Contributions from Fischer and Stephens are unintelligible. There's only the flash of the paddle, Bobby's soothing voice and my warm space. Before long I'm flying in an untroubled sky, Bobby sailing in formation beside me.

I don't know how long this goes on. What brings me down is a wet cold fire consuming my ass. I come to my senses with the smell of rubbing alcohol in my nose, the sound of a spray bottle being pumped. I scream into the gag again but can find no relief. Damn, it burns! I drop my head to Bobby's shoulder and whimper.

"Fuck," I hear Stephens say. I try to raise my head to look at him but the effort is just too much. I smell cigar smoke in the room but I don't know who's smoking. Maybe it's just my ass.

"Don't blow yet, buddy," Fisher says. "There's more to come."

With that, as if on cue, I feel someone's weight on the foot of the bed. I try to regain my senses. This is important. I manage to pull it together long enough to look into Bobby's eyes. There's absolute support there. I realize he's been accepting some of my energy, reacting for my body on autopilot.

Warm grease is spread across my asshole. I snap to attention, look to the side. Stephens and Fischer have their dicks out. I see Fischer stroking his. That must be Master Burt on the bed. He's directly behind me, also straddling Bobby, trapping my bare feet and calves with his boots. A finger penetrates me, then another. I breathe deeply and relax. Here we go again. There's the sound of a cellophane package being opened -- another condom? -- and a moment later Master Burt is pressing his cock into my asshole. He drives himself all the way home in one stroke, demanding, confident. When he's done he rests there with his pubes tickling my sore ass cheeks.

"Uh-huh," Master Burt says. "Damn fine hole you got there, boy."

I whimper a bit more, steeling myself for the fuck to come.

Master Burt grabs my tied hands. He pulls his cock back and comes home again, starts the fuck while holding onto my wrists. I inhale and obey his rhythm. In and out, in and out, my wrists used like reins. The fuck is easy and feels good almost at once. I imagine him penetrating me, claiming my ass, filling me and making me complete. This is my rightful place.

Stephens and Fischer are enjoying the show but their voices seem distant and unreal, like they're watching us on television. Master Burt is a skilled top, his rhythm regular and confident, just a little emphasis at the end of each stroke. Bobby is a lucky boy indeed if he gets to experience this regularly. Bobby! I'd completely forgotten him. Now I realize he's moving beneath me, grunting, lifting his pelvis to move my ass in response to his Master's fuck. Oh my God this is the most incredible thing I've ever experienced! It's like I'm being fucked and yet the bed itself is joining in on the action, warm and sweaty and wriggling. I nuzzle Bobby's ear, grunting. I clench down on my hole to give Master Burt an extra bit of pleasure, move and shift my ass. Fuck me! Fuck me, Sir! Damn, I love being used! Bobby grunts and Master Burt keeps a tight rein on my arms, driving myself home.

I hear groaning elsewhere in the room, Fischer shooting his load. It doesn't matter. Nothing matters except the sweaty pile of meat on the bed. Bobby is rocking his pelvis against mine, slowly jerking my cock off. Oh my God I don't know how much longer I can hold myself in! I buck my head, snort and spray sweat off my nose. Master Burt has got my ass wide open now. It's like he's rubbing his dick against his boy and my rectum just happens to be in the way. I could take a fist with no problem right now, a whole fucking subway train if I wanted! Master Burt's moaning. I rock myself against him, stroke his palms with my bound hands. I want to cry out from sheer joy. The three of us are in a warm wet universe of flesh and restraint and the salty odor of sweat. We stay there on the pinnacle like a circus act working without a net. I wonder who will go first.

It's Bobby. His pelvic thrusts become sharp jabs and he finally screams against his gag, spewing cum from his rock hard dick. His jizz fills the space between us, warm and slick like contact cement, coupling me to his orgasm. It's all I need to send me over the top. I cry out, strain and buck and scream against everything holding me back, empty two days worth of cum and frustration all over Bobby's stomach. My gut convulses, mindlessly, and this is all Master But needs to shoot his own load. He shouts out loud -- not words but an orgasm translated into a masculine grunt. I can feel his cock pulse deep within my ass, his juice filling up the condom that separates us, dripping down around the outside. He holds tight against my ass as his body shudders.

Time has ceased. The three of us are one, fused by sweat, cum. We breath. We drip. We are.

And then it's done. Master Burt collapses onto my back, covering me, his weight pressing me against his boy. Between gasps for breath he tenderly kisses my shoulder. His cock slips from my asshole, warm and wet and softening. I feel jizz drip down the back of my thigh.

I can't say how long we stay that way, spent and exhausted, seeking gaps in the rhythm big enough in which to breathe. I sweat and absorb. Endorphins fade. I become aware that my hands are screaming from the ropes, that my neck hurts, that my eyes are stinging from salt. Master Burt rises from the pile and staggers off the bed. I hear his boots hit the floor, the sound of a kiss from one of the other men. No one speaks. Hands reach for the bonds around my wrists, untie them, slowly bring my arms over my head. My shoulders cry out with new pain but I don't mind. I stay there, collapsed against Bobby while my neck is released from his. I have no will of my own, no power. I simply respond and move in the direction I'm prodded. I lay fetal beside Bobby, still gagged, untied but more helpless than ever.

Master Burt returns to the bed and kneels above his boy, slowly runs a hand along Bobby's arms, legs and chest. Bobby looks up at his master with adoring eyes, his skin turned to goose-flesh from the touch. Master Burt dredges his hand through the gobs of loosening cum that have pooled atop Bobby's stomach, lifts the cum to Bobby's face, smears it against his cheeks and along the gag beneath his nose. Bobby closes his eyes and inhales deeply, filling himself with the scent. Master Burt collects more jizz and applies it to Bobby's forehead, his close-cropped hair, his chest and nipples. He works the cream into every exposed square inch. Bobby lays there still bound, eyes closed, arcing himself to receive his Master's attention. When the cum is dry and sticky, Bobby's breaths having slowed, Master Burt bends down and tenderly kisses each of Bobby's closed eyes.

Hands find me. I realize I have been drifting toward sleep. Bobby is untied now and sitting on the other side of the bed, his master beside him. He slowly raises his ass and shits out a large silicone butt plug.

"Move yourself into the center of the bed, boy." It's Stephens' voice in my ear. I do as I am told, wriggling weakly into position. They tie me spread-eagle to the bed again, similar to last night.

Exactly where I need to be.

I open my eyes slowly. Fisher, Stephens and Master Burt are fully clothed again, looking at me with a mixture of superiority and fatherly protection. Bobby stands there too, naked except for collar and padded wrist restraints. The restraints are connected with long lengths of light gauge chain, enough for him to be comfortable but also enough for him to remember his place.

His gag has been removed and I see he's got his head buried against Master Burt's furry chest.

Stephens leans in close and looks at me. "You comfortable, boy?"

I smell smoke on his breath. "Mmmmmmph," I say against the gag, a sound of contentment and weariness.

"Goooood, boy. You'll make me proud yet."

I want to, Sir. I want to very much.

"Okay," Master Burt says.

Bobby stands up straight and looks at him, ready to receive instruction.

"Time for you boys to go to sleep," he says. "You've had enough fun for one day."

"Yes, Sir," Bobby says.

Master Burt raises Bobby's chin with a finger and leans in for a tender kiss. I look at Stephens and I wish we could do the same. But it's not to be. Bobby crawls into bed beside me and curls up, his head on my chest. I see that his legs are also restrained by another long length of chain. The men turn the lights out, take one glance back before shutting the door and leaving Bobby and I alone in the darkness. Something seems important. There's something I should do, some opportunity I should seize, but it's so difficult to think.

Finally I realize what it is. Bobby is relatively unrestrained. He could untie me. I could escape.

I grunt against the gag. Bobby doesn't respond so I do it again, louder but still weary.

"Shhhhhhh," Bobby says against my chest. I smell my cum in his hair.

I grunt again, more insistent. I try to put more energy into it but I've got so little to spare. Even as I struggle, sleep is rising over me like the tide.

"Shhhhhh," Bobby says again. "Just sleep."

His advice sounds so logical, so right. I flail my arms but I can tell it's no use. My grunts are no more than half-hearted whimpers. I'm floating away with Bobby curled up beside me. I feel warm and comfortable and in this moment nothing else could possibly matter.

A Boner Book

Day Three

I wake slowly and easily. Bobby is curled up asleep beside me, his head on my chest. I feel different, relaxed, comfortable in the ropes. The room is the same as before -- dull sunlight and faded wallpaper, the stale scents of cigar and lube in the air -- but strangely I feel contented, as if everything is just as it should be. They must have drugged me. Either that, or I've just come to accept the situation.

Bobby is beautiful. It makes me feel powerful to have him sleep beside me this way. Master Burt must experience this every night. I listen to the sounds in the ranch, try to pick out his or anyone else's voice but I can't. There's only a diffuse male presence. I relax and simply enjoy the moment.

Sometime later men approach down the hallway outside. The door opens and I look up to see Officer Stephens and Master Burt enter. Stephens is wearing Wranglers, cowboy boots and a white T-shirt stained with motor grease. He's carrying the familiar drink bottle. Master Burt is dressed in yesterday's boots and jeans along with an olive green T-shirt.

Bobby stirs at the sound of boots in the room. He blinks against the morning light, then his eyes focus on his master. He slips out of bed, wordlessly and without hesitation, and walks with downcast eyes toward Master Burt, the chain around his ankles jangling. Master Burt waits at the center of the room, and Bobby kneels before him, kisses the fly of his jeans, efficiently opens them and carefully removes the penis. He holds the head of the soft penis against his lips and kisses it, lingering and breathing in the smell of his master's crotch. All this has the practiced air of a morning ritual.

"Now that's training," Stephens says, half-smile on his face.

Master Burt nods. "Bobby's a good boy, aren't you, Bobby?" He pats the back of Bobby's head.

Bobby lays his head against his master's crotch. His eyes are closed with contentment. "Yes, Sir. I'm a good boy, Sir."

"All right, boy, put that away. I'm hungry."

"Yes, Sir!" Bobby carefully returns the penis to Master Burt's pants and buttons up the fly.

"You need me for anything in here, bud?" Burt asks Stephens.

Stephens looks at me. "Naw. I doubt fuckhole here is going to give me any trouble."

"Okay." Master Burt snaps his fingers and Bobby stands quickly. Burt removes a key from his pocket and releases Bobby from the chains, which Bobby collects. "Come on, boy," he turns to go and Bobby follows him out of the room.

Officer Stephens looks at me. "I hope you've been taking notes, boy. I expect that kind of obedience from you, especially tomorrow when we'll be having guests."

"Efff, furr," I say around the gag.

He approaches me, rubs my head. "Good boy. Time for your breakfast." He removes the gag and sets it aside. I take the opportunity to swallow and run my tongue around the inside of my mouth, free for the first time in hours. It feels like there's several inches of fuzz growing on my teeth. Officer Stephens fills the drink bottle with piss and I drain it down with barely a thought. He orders me to stay while he unties my hands and feet, then he helps me to sit up and swing my legs off the edge of the bed. While I'm doing this, I feel a sharp stabbing pain in my right shoulder, and I flinch.

Stephens freezes. "What was that, boy?"

I look up at him. "A pain in my shoulder, Sir. It took me by surprise."

"Can you move it?"

I try. "It doesn't hurt anymore, Sir."

"Let's have a look at it." His concern seems at once both genuine and inconceivable. He tests the flexibility of the joint, commanding me to rotate my arm. The pain does not reappear. "We're going to watch that, boy. You tell me or Fischer the moment it doesn't feel right. You understand?"

I don't respond, simply look at him incredulous.

"I expect you to answer my questions, boy!"

"Sir, yes sir! The moment it doesn't feel right, SIR!"

He nods. "That's better. Now get your sorry ass out of bed. We've already wasted enough time here."

He takes me to the enema room for another clean out, gives me another liter of orange juice. I'm dumbstruck by his reaction to my shoulder. Why would he treat me that way? Is he just showing concern for his property? I want to ask him, to understand, but there's a wall between us that I don't dare breach. Stephens goes about his tasks with a certain distance. Suddenly I realize he's not a natural sadist like Fischer. Despite kidnapping me he seems to hold the warm regard a master should have for his boy, but he also knows that fear and punishment are some of his more useful tools. I've no time to ponder this as I am given my sneakers and a jock and taken to the gym. No buttplug up my ass today. I am to work back and biceps, and we begin with deadlifts. Stephens keeps the paddle close by. I smell bacon and eggs frying in the kitchen and it makes me salivate. I can't keep focussed on the weight. All I can think of is real food and it nearly drives me crazy.

I work. I sweat. Stephens watches my form and uses the paddle, sparingly but hard. I feel intense drive to do a good job. Master Burt enters with Bobby just as we're finishing up. He is shirtless with a pair of sweatpants, USMC logo on the side. Bobby is wearing a jock and short black boots. He stands respectfully behind his master.

"If you don't mind," Master Burt says, "I'd like to work my boy."

"Don't mind at all," Stephens says. "Can you watch the fuckhole for a little while?"

"Yeah, no problem."

Stephens looks at me. "Go back into your bedroom, boy, and bring me last night's gag and the lengths of rope and blindfold from the night table on the right. You think you can do that without fucking it up?"

I nod. "Sir, yes sir!"

"Get to it, then. Don't make me wait or I'll tie you up tighter."

I leave the gym. I'm free and unsupervised! Should I make a break for it? I know where the front door is. . .

But then what? There's no one around for miles, and the sun would cook me pretty damn fast wearing nothing but a jock and sneakers. What are the chances they left the keys in their vehicles? I find the rope no problem and hesitate just a moment before returning to the gym. It's not the right time. Tomorrow, with more people should be better. I'll wait.

I present the items to Stephens. He orders me to stand feet together with hands at sides, and he proceeds to tie me up with Master Burt's help. First he lashes my arms securely in place and then ties my legs together, orders me to remain rigid while Master Burt topples me forward. Officer Stephens lowers me to the mat, bends my legs at the knees and ties my ankles to a length of rope about my neck. I'm left in a modified hog-tie on the gym floor, the silicone gag and the blindfold completing the treatment.

Stephens places his boot atop my back then. I can feel the dusty leather sole and sharp Western heel. "You comfortable there, fuckhole?"

"Emmmph phur." I force through the gag.

"Very well then. Room's all yours, Burt."

"Thank you."

Stephens leaves us, and Master Burt and Bobby begin a workout. I am ignored. Master Burt's attitude toward fitness is similar to Stephens' -- a workout should be equal parts physical training and S/M scene. It's difficult to tell whether he drives himself or Bobby harder, but hearing the two of them strain against the weights it's no wonder Bobby has such a wonderful physique. Master Burt must have created his own muscle-bottom. They're working legs -- heavy by sound of it --and Burt seems to favor supersetting everything with squats. Bobby whimpers through the upper ranges of his sets but always completes them.

I lay there on the floor, occasionally straining against the ropes just to enjoy the feel of them around my body. The grit on the floor mixes with my sweat, forming an abrasive paste beneath my chest, crotch and thighs. It's painful and wonderful all at once, especially against my abused nipples. The rubber odor of the mat is strong in my nose, and denied sight, I form a mental picture of Bobby and Burt working out. My dick oscillates between semi-soft and rock hard.

Eventually someone enters the room and places his boot on my ass. I assume it's Stephens, but I'm wrong.

"Good morning, Bud," Fischer says. I assume he's talking to Master Burt.

"Morning," Burt grunts. He finishes his set and approaches. It feels like they shake hands. "I was just working the boy here."

"I see that."

Bobby grinds out another set.

"Shoot," Fischer says, "that's all the weight you got him doing?"

"We're ramping down now," Burt says.

"That's no way to work," Fischer says. "You need to go until they collapse."

Master Burt doesn't respond. It sounds like he's doing another set.

"Shit," Fischer continues, "when we worked the fuckhole here the other day he went heavier than that."

What the hell is he doing?

"Yeah?" Master Burt asks. He sounds irritated.

"Fuck yeah. Don't get me wrong, Bud. Your boy looks good and all but you got him doing a pussy set there."

Master Burt lets that go.

"You know," Fischer continues. "I got twenty bucks here says the fuckhole here can kick Bobby's ass."

"Come again?"

"You heard me," Fischer says. "Twenty bucks and our little fuckhole here takes Bobby down." He taps his boot on my ass for emphasis. I start wriggling on the floor then, and Fischer increases the pressure until I stop.

I hear the sound of a barbell drop. The floor shakes. "You're fuckin' on."

Oh, no.

"That's an easy twenty bucks," Fischer says.

Master Burt comes closer. "But what say we make this a little more interesting?"

"Like what?"

"Like winner fucks the loser. I ain't seen Bobby fuck a piece of meat in a long while. Figure he deserves a treat."

"Shoot! Only two things gonna get fucked here -- that pussy boy over there and your wallet!"

Master Burt chuckles. "We'll see about that."

I exhale and drop my head. I don't want to fight Bobby. Suddenly the ropes feel constricting. It's hard to breathe.

Someone else enters the room. "You starting trouble in here?" It's Stephens.

"Just making a friendly wager," Fischer says. "The boy here can take Bobby down. Winner fucks the loser, and I got twenty bucks on it."

"What are you doing committing my piece of ass?"

"Look," Fischer says, "you got nothing to worry about. Even if the boy loses -- which he won't -- Princess Tinymeat over there ain't gonna do any damage."

Bobby is no Princess Tinymeat.

Stephens sighs heavily. "You a party to this, Burt?"

"My boy don't take shit from no one except me."

There's a long pause. "All right," Stephens says, "but you

listen to me, Fischer. You get the fuckhole injured and I swear, I *swear*, you'll be my piece of ass tomorrow."

"You got nothing to worry about, Bud," Fischer says.

"Dumb ass!" Stephen mutters on his way out of the room.

I can't believe this.

Fischer unties me, removes the gag and the blindfold. I see he's wearing his uniform again -- he must have just come off duty. Damn, he's sexy! I almost forget everything that's happened over the past few days and touch my dick to start jacking off, like he's a fucking jpeg I downloaded off the internet. Fischer orders me to stand. I do, rubbing my wrists and arms until my hands lose their numbness.

Across the room Master Burt has his hands on Bobby's shoulders. He's looking into his eyes, giving Bobby instruction. Bobby nods occasionally, intense and focussed.

There's a mat stacked against the wall. Fischer orders me to bring it to the center of the room, and when I unfold it, I see it's got a wrestling circle printed on it. Bobby helps me position it. I try to catch his eye, to see how he feels about this, but he won't meet mine. He's shut himself down. Stephens returns to the room just as Bobby kneels on the mat, facing the center. I don't want to but I don't see any way around it, so I join him there. We face each other.

"All right, boys," Stephens says, "you two be careful. I don't want to hear any snapping joints. If one of you wants to submit, you just holler 'GIVE', you got me?"

"Yes, Sir!" Bobby says quickly.

"Yes, Sir," I say. Bobby's looking dead forward and won't meet my gaze. What did Burt tell him?

"Best two out of three, boys," Stephens says. He glances at Fischer. "Winner fucks the loser."

"Okay boys," Master Burt says. "Clench."

Bobby and I lean forward and clamp our hands on each other's shoulders. Bobby's shoulders are warm and slicked with sweat, the muscles beneath rock hard. I suddenly feel very small and weak. He's still limbered up from his workout, where-as I spent the last hour hog-tied on the cold floor. I've never really paid attention to sport wrestling but it's obvious I need to get him on his back or push him out of the ring. Winner fucks the loser? Well, I *was* thinking that I wanted to nail that pretty ass of his. Maybe Bobby will let me win -- he doesn't seem aggressive enough to top.

Bobby leans in some more, and I do the same until our foreheads are touching. I can smell bacon on his breath. Son of a bitch.

"Let me win," I whisper. "I'm a good top."

Bobby focuses on my eyes for the first time. "No."

"Why?"

"Break!" Fischer shouts.

Before I know it I'm being pushed backward. I lose my balance and see the overhead lights streak across my vision. Bobby lands atop me and knocks the wind from my chest.

"Shit!" Fischer says. "Match!"

Master Burt is chuckling. Stephens shakes his head.

Bobby rises from me and offers me a hand up. I ignore it and get up myself. Damn him! He didn't even give me a chance! I guess this is for real. We get back into position and clasp shoulders. I've been fucked by everyone but the dog for the last two days and I better wise up if I want to avoid getting it again. I'm not warmed up, which works against me, but I know Bobby just did a killer leg workout. I can even see him wince when he moves. My legs are rested, so that's my best chance.

We meet again. This time he meets my eyes. "I can't let anyone but my master fuck me," he whispers. "I'm sorry."

Fischer yells BREAK and I detonate my legs. Bobby tries to overpower me again but it doesn't work a second time. Instead I push him backward. His legs crumple beneath him, and he lands first on his ass, then on his back, his head outside the ring.

"Ha!" Fischer yells. I hear Master Burt swear.

Bobby is looking up at me, shock in his eyes. "I'm sorry too," I mumble. And I mean it. But this is for real and I don't want to get fucked again. I go back onto my knees and offer him my hand. He takes it. We trudge back to the center of the mat, turn and face one another.

"How are you boys doing?" Stephens asks.

"Good, Sir," Bobby says.

"Great, Sir," I say.

Fischer chuckles. "Heh! That's what I'm talking about. Hey, Burt!"

"What," Master Burt says sourly.

"How about that twenty bucks becomes fifty?"

"You're fuckin' on."

"All right," Stephens says. "Let's get this over with. You boys ready?"

We nod at one another. "Yes, Sir," we say.

"Break!" Stephens says.

No surprises this time. I fight. Bobby fights. But we know each others weaknesses now. I jam my torso into Bobby's stomach and piston him backward. He's ready for this and twists himself off to the side. I overbalance and end up on all fours. Bobby's on top of me lightning quick. I did a back workout this morning, and Bobby watched the end of that so he knows to concentrate on my arms. I can't keep them in position and I go down with my chin on the mat. I sweep my legs backward, looking to knock him off balance. It works and he goes down on his ass. I turn to face him as quickly as I can. I've got momentum on my side, and Bobby's legs are folded beneath him, so I aim high. I picture him toppling over backward, but it doesn't happen that way. Instead, Bobby melts out of my way as I'm coming forward. I never would have thought he could move that fast! I'm still barely touching the mat when he's beneath my side and pushing upward. The gym rotates. Before I know it I crash down backward onto the mat. Surprise and the force of the landing knock the breath from my chest, and then Bobby is atop me, covering me with his warm bulk.

"Match!" Master Burt yells. "Ha!"

"Shit!" Fischer says.

I'm staring up at the lights swimming overhead. I lost. I lost to Bobby.

He hoists himself off me and kneels on the mat. He offers me his hand, and this time I take it, his grip warm and strong. I come to my own knees directly in front of him, stare into his handsome face. I place my hands around the small of his back, lightly, and none of the men in the room complain.

Fischer walks over to Master Burt and hands him several bills. "Damn," he says.

"Thank you," Master Burt says. "I do believe we got ourselves a floor show here."

We both look at him.

"Yeah," says Stephens. "Let's get this over with. I don't want to lose the whole damn day."

I look to Bobby, unsure of what happens next.

"Lay on your back, boy," Master Burt says to Bobby. "Let him get you hard first."

"Sir! Yes Sir!" Bobby drops himself back onto his elbows, extends his legs and looks up at me. I lean my face down, nuzzle the black fabric of his jockstrap with my cheek. It smells wonderful, warm and moist, salty and masculine all at once. The scruff of my unshaven cheeks catches abrasively against the jock and the sensation prompts Bobby's cock to swell. I look up at him. The fur on his belly is foreshortened into a dark mat.

There's uncertainty in his eyes.

I realize suddenly that I'm going to enjoy this. Not only did I cost Fischer fifty bucks, but I get to have sex with this wonderful man.

I pull aside the elastic fabric of the jock pouch, revealing the full cock just beneath. Another wave of musk hits me then and I bury my nose in the space between his thigh and his dick. I inhale deeply, feel my own cock strain against my jockstrap. In a moment I've got Bobby's cock free, my hand wrapped around it from below and cradling the balls. I open my mouth and slowly take it all inside, caressing his cock with my tongue, burying my nose in his remaining pubes. Bobby moans and I feel tension melt away from his muscles.

"Gooood boy," I hear Master Burt say. Whether he's speaking to me or Bobby I have no idea.

I slowly suck Bobby's cock. I don't have to work to make him hard -- that's already done. Instead I concentrate on taking his meat all the way inside my mouth, stroking his balls in rhythm. Bobby luxuriates on the mat like it's satin, spreads himself out, strokes his own nipples. I'm dimly aware of the other men in the room. I concentrate on Bobby's cock while Bobby is passive beneath me. He moans but doesn't interact, doesn't grab my head to direct the blow job, doesn't take charge.

"All right, boy," Master Burt says. There's an edge to his voice.

Bobby opens his eyes and immediately directs his attention to his master.

"Let's finish this up," Master Burt continues.

"Yes, Sir!" Bobby responds. He comes up on his elbows and looks at me. I meet his gaze, my mouth stuffed with his cock.

Show time, I think. I pull my mouth away from his cock, give his balls a firm squeeze as I come up to a kneeling position on the mat. A condom package lands atop Bobby's abs, and a moment later, a small jar of lube lands beside us as well.

"Go to it, boys," says Officer Stephens. "You stay on your back, Bobby. I want to see the boy here fuck himself."

I glance quickly at Stephens, standing there with his hands on hips. It's a pleasure to perform for this man.

I slick Bobby's cock up with the lube, open the condom package and unroll the latex. Some more lube goes on top like pancake syrup. Bobby lies there looking up at me. Is he worried he'll lose the erection? How long has it been since Master Burt let him have some ass? Will he even enjoy this? No time for questions -- we've got a job to do. I squat above Bobby's midsection, reach down to adjust his penis and slowly lower myself over it. The head tickles my sphincter, pressures it. I realize that I should have lubed up my ass, but I've been fucked so many times over the past two days I don't suppose it matters. No sense procrastinating. I lower my ass and take Bobby's cock fully inside me, gasping. This position is always too much work. It looks better than it feels, which I guess is the whole point of this anyway. I fuck myself on Bobby's pole, up and down, balancing myself with my hands resting on my knees. After Thursday's leg workout the stretch in my thighs feels damn good anyway, and my hole blossoms with warmth, like it wasn't happy without a cock inside it. Bobby returns to his passive mode, closes his eyes and stretches his hands above his head.

I slow my rhythm, reach out and take his hands. He locks his eyes on mine and I resume my work. I hold him with my gaze, bring him along. He starts to move his hips, compensating, lengthening the stroke. *Now* we're together.

We go on like this for a while. I slowly ease myself onto Bobby's cock, up again, down. It's comfortable but tiring. Eventually it seems to me that while we're both enjoying the company, the action, no one's really getting close to shooting. That won't satisfy these men. Bobby won't take the initiative though, so I lower myself fully onto his dick, resting my weight on his pelvis and wincing as the head pushes deep into my gut. I lean backward until I'm laying on the mat. Bobby lifts himself onto his knees and bears his weight down on me in the classic missionary position. He fucks me, tentative at first but gaining in strength. I stroke his thick forearms, reach around to caress his lower back, up to brush his nipples. His rhythm quickens. We've created our own little sanctuary here on the mat, bounded by our bodies and the sound of our breathing. Bobby closes his eyes. I continue to stroke his nipples, pinch, pull them. He responds by fucking me harder, his mouth hanging open. He's so damn beautiful! I stroke his back, nuzzle his rock-hard forearm. He whimpers, his face inches from mine.

"Yeah, boy," I say, quiet so that only he can hear. "Yeah, you like that asshole?"

He whimpers again.

"Fuck it, boy. Fuck it and make your master proud."

Bobby responds by nailing my ass harder.

"Yeah. Such a good boy, aren't you?"

"Yes, Sir," he breathes. "I'm a good boy."

I pinch his nipples, hard this time. "Fuck that asshole, boy. Fuck that asshole like you own it."

"Yes, Sir!" he grunts. He's into it now, punishing my rectum. I grit my teeth to block out the pain, reach back and slap his ass. "Do it, boy! Shoot your load and make your master proud."

"Yes, Sir. Oh, yes sir. Thank you, Sir."

I pinch his nipples hard enough to make him wince. "Fuck it, boy. That's right. Rape that asshole."

"Yes sir! Yes sir!" His legs are bucking now, uncontrolled. "Thank you, Sir!"

"Do it, boy. I'm going to give you to a count of ten. Ten, nine, eight, seven. . ."

"Uhhhh," Bobby moans. "Uhhh. . ."

"Six, five. . . C'mon boy. Let me see it."

Bobby shouts something unintelligible, his eyes shut tight.

"Four. . . three. . ."

He cries out.

"Two. . . one!"

"AH!"

His orgasm seizes him, smashes him, reduces him to spasming muscle and sweaty skin. Each stroke is punctuated by a shout, each less intense than the last. I hug myself to him, bury my face in his chest, pull him close and leave no space between us. He drops his head to my shoulder and weeps great, racking sobs. I lower my ass to the mat and his cock plops out. His legs tremble and collapse and he slumps atop me, chest heaving, tears mingling with sweat to roll down my cheek.

"Good boy," I whisper into his ear. "You done good, boy."

His sobs erupt anew. I stoke his back, hug him tighter, whisper softly to him. We're slick and warm and together. Alone in the room. Alone in the world.

For a brief moment. That's all.

But it's enough.

I'm aware of movement nearby, someone standing on the wrestling mat. I look to the side and see black boots. Master Burt has kneeled down and started stroking Bobby's back. I quickly remove my hands.

"Good boy," Master Burt says. "You done me real proud."

"Thank you, Sir," Bobby says around his gasps. He doesn't open his eyes, doesn't look at his master. "Thank you."

"Gooood boy," Master Burt croons. "Gooood boy. . ."

"God fucking damn," Stephens says. I look over, see the crotch of his jeans wet with pre-cum.

"That was almost worth fifty bucks," Fischer says.

We are left to lay with one another for several minutes. Bobby's breathing slows and eventually he opens his eyes. Master Burt is standing beside us now, stroking the bulge in his sweat pants. Bobby looks up at him. He pulls himself from our embrace and kneels beside his master, lays his cheek against Master Burt's crotch. Bobby's cock is softening. He reaches down and slips off the condom, stuffs his meat back into his jock. "Thank you, Sir."

"Damn," Master Burt says. "You got me going."

"Yes, Sir," Bobby says, his eyes closed.

Master Burt rubs Bobby's head. He looks to Stephens. "Hey, bud. You mind if I use the fuckhole a little more?"

Stephens shakes his head. "Not at all. That's what he's here for."

Master Burt looks down at me, a smile on his lips. He pats Bobby's head, sharply, and Bobby snaps to attention. "Go into the next room," Master Burt tells him, "and get me one of those chairs. Be quick about it."

"Yes, Sir!" Bobby stands, hesitating just a moment when his legs quiver beneath him.

His master steadies him. "You okay, boy?"

"Yes, Sir! I'm fine, Sir, just a little shaky. I'll be right back!" Bobby slips from the room, returns a moment later with a wooden chair.

Master Burt snaps his fingers and points. "Over there."

Bobby does as he is told. I am ordered to go sit in the chair, and then Master Burt takes the ropes from the floor and ties me up. First come my legs, then my torso. He crosses my wrists behind the chair back but Stephens whispers something into his ear and Master Burt relents, tying my hands to the vertical back supports instead. My ass is sloppy and wet, slicking up the chair seat. The ropes get me hard all over again and my dick strains at the jock pouch. Master Burt orders Bobby to remove his jock, which he does, and then he orders me to open my mouth. He shoves the jock into my mouth. It's salty and wet and faintly sweet from the lube. Next duct tape is wrapped around my head and mouth several times, securing the jock in place. Afterward, Master Burt stands back to look me over. The bulge in his pants is even bigger.

Fischer chuckles. "That's pretty."

Master Burt laughs. "You ain't seen nothing yet." He looks at Bobby, who stands naked beside him, hands clasped behind his back and eyes down. Master Burt snaps his fingers and points at the floor in front of me. "Stand there, boy, facing the chair."

Bobby does so. I look up into his face, hoping to catch his eyes but he keeps his gaze directed downward. His dick is semi-hard, still oozing juice from our fuck only minutes ago. Master Burt bends Bobby over until his face is just inches from mine. Bobby supports himself on my bound shoulders. Master Burt caresses Bobby's ass for several seconds, then spanks it hard. Bobby jerks but doesn't cry out. I feel his exhaled breath on my nipples.

"Damn," Stephens says. He's standing just behind me. "You're gonna make me fuckin' shoot my load, bud."

"Occupational hazard," Master Burt says. He walks over to where Bobby and I wrestled a moment ago and retrieves the bottle of lube from the floor. Bobby glances in that direction, and he shuts his eyes tight and parts his lips. He knows what's coming. I grunt encouragement and lean my head forward to nuzzle his cheek. We're in this together, man.

Master Burt is behind his boy now. I see him push his sweatpants down until the waistband is around his knees. He lubes himself up and drops the bottle, grabs Bobby firmly at the waist and pushes himself inside in one merciless movement. Bobby gasps and cries out. His eyes scrunch tighter.

"Yeah, boy," Master Burt says. "Give me what's mine."

"Yes Sir!" Bobby chokes out.

Master Burt pulls himself out and comes back home, out and back, out and back, settling into a nice slow rhythm. I look past Bobby to watch him, so damn handsome as he fucks his boy. My dick is raging hard, straining at the limits of my jock. If only I could touch my dick I'd cum instantly! Bobby hugs himself to me tighter as his ass is reamed. I crane my head forward and rub it against his head, humming softly.

Now I see Fischer and Stephens walk into view from either side. Stephens has his fat dick out now, stroking it slowly and watching the show while Fischer is content to simply rub the bulge in his dark gray uniform pants. Master Burt keeps his attention focused on his boy. His thrusts have gotten faster, more violent, and he reaches forward to grab Bobby's shoulder. I move my head out of the way.

"Yeah, bud," Stephens says, stroking himself faster.

Master Burt is punishing Bobby's ass now. I hear the slap

of his balls against the back of Bobby's thighs. Bobby is whimpering, his body held firmly. I stretch my chin upward, struggle to swallow around the jock shoved into my mouth. This is like watching a really hot porn movie but being unable to touch my cock. I kick at the rope holding my legs, try to move my hands but nothing works. I'm held fast.

Master Burt grunts at the end of each stroke, viciously nailing Bobby's ass. Bobby hugs himself to me. I can't see his eyes but I'm sure he's someplace far away, just as I was last night when Master Burt pounded me. And suddenly Master Burt's grunts turn into shouts. His rhythm has gone all loose and sloppy and before I know it he's spent himself. He bends forward and hugs himself to Bobby, chest heaving, eyes shut tight. These two just did a leg workout and then each pounded some ass. I can't imagine how tired they feel.

"Damn," Stephens says, shaking his head in admiration. His rod is still hard but he's stopped stroking it, apparently intent on saving his orgasm. He glances at his watch.

Master Burt pulls himself from Bobby, stands up straight and pulls his pants back up to his waist. He snaps his fingers and Bobby immediately lets go of me, turns and kneels on the floor beside his master. He rests his head against his master's thigh. Master Burt strokes his sweaty hair.

Burt, his chest still heaving, looks at Stephens. "I gotta thank you for the hospitality. This has been just great."

"You and me both, Burt." They shake hands. "Is it getting late for you?"

"Yeah."

"You want to shower?" Fischer asks.

Master Burt looks down at Bobby. "Naw, I think I'll leave the boy ripe. Make things more interesting when we stop later."

"Heh!" Officer Stephens says. "You're always thinking ahead. You want the jock back?" He points at my duct-taped mouth.

Master Burt looks me up and down, considers. "Naw. Let him keep it as a souvenir."

Stephens, Fischer, and Master Burt laugh at that.

The men collect their belongings. Bobby moves the exercise mat back against the wall, and on his way past me he glances quickly in my direction. I almost miss it. In an instant they're gone and the door is shut. I'm alone. I hear voices in the house for the next ten minutes or so. Before long there's the sound of a motorcycle firing to life and driving away.

They're gone, just like they'd never been here. My situation is no different than yesterday morning -- hell, it never was any different. So why do I feel so alone? Why do I feel so damn sad?

I struggle against the ropes. I've always enjoyed bondage, and I know that some tops tie you up with just enough slack so that you could get free if you just work at it. I test and pull and try. Master Burt didn't intend for me to get myself free. This frustrates me and I find myself working all the harder. My wrists and ankles ache from the pressure and I'm sweating all over again. My sloppy ass cheeks slide on the wooden seat. My tongue has memorized every ridge and fold of the jockstrap jammed into my mouth. It reminds me of Bobby, and for that I'm grateful. Finally I give up and slump into the chair.

I doze. The doors in this house seem solid and well-built. I can hear very little through them. Fischer and Stephens must still be around but there's no way to be sure.

Eventually the door opens and someone enters. I snap awake but don't turn around to view him. He slaps the back of my head as he passes. That's Fischer's style. Sure enough, it's him. He stands beside my chair and regards me. He's bare chested, wearing black POLICE ATHLETIC sweatpants, army boots and black-leather workout gloves. I look up at him, examine the bushy moustache, those cold eyes, the hairy chest and the snake tattoo.

Fischer chuckles to himself and then walks over to the exercise equipment. He stretches and warms up, begins a chest routine. Before long he's got a good sheen of sweat going. I can watch the show from my vantage point in the chair, my jock pouch bulging. Fischer is a walking fantasy, from the uniform to the fur to the cigars to the attitude. I suddenly feel overcome with. . . what? I don't know, submission? I'm grateful to these men. I love these men. I want to stay with them forever.

"I got some plans for you, Fuckhole," Fischer says. He's grinding through concentration curls. I watch him closely but it's several minutes before he elaborates. He transfers the dumbbell to the other arm, looks squarely at me. "Stephens has to go on duty tonight." He curls his arm up and down, up and down, straining against the weight. The left bicep, encircled with the snake tattoo, bulges. "He's going to leave you in my care." He drops the weight, stands and walks over to me. A runner of sweat dribbles down his chest, off his nipple and onto my thigh. I look up into his eyes, helpless.

"Your ass is mine tonight, fuckmeat, and Officer Stephens won't be around to protect you. If I were you, I'd start worrying right about now."

My dick goes soft.

Officer Fischer finishes his workout but doesn't share any more of his plans. When he's done he returns to me in the chair. "Hold still, fucker." He steadies my scalp with one hand and unravels the duct-tape with the other, unceremoniously pulling away the final layer adhered to my skin and hair. I cry out from the pain, which only elicits another chuckle from him. He orders me to spit out the jockstrap, which I do. He finishes untying me, orders me to put the ropes and chair back where they belong. Bobby's jockstrap is stored with the ropes. Then he marches me into the enema room and showers me down, once again with the abrasive soap. I'm drying off when Officer Stephens enters the room. He's changed into his uniform, dress shoes instead of boots, tight leather gloves and fully loaded duty belt. He's not wearing his Stetson. The sight of him in uniform is comforting and erotic all at once, but then I remember that he's leaving me alone with Fischer tonight. Stephens is carrying something made of leather.

"You got him all cleaned up?" Stephens asks.

"Yep. All presentable now."

"Good. Come here, boy," he says to me. I approach with the damp towel and stand before him, eyes down. He inspects me for a moment, then lifts my chin with a light touch of his gloved hand. He looks into my eyes. "I have to go on duty, but don't worry. Officer Fischer is going to take good care of you."

Fischer chuckles again.

"Yes, Sir," I say.

"Good boy. Here, I got something for you. Put this on." He holds out the leather for me. I see its a pair of shorts equipped with belts around the waist, right thigh and left thigh. There's also an unusual number of snaps and rings. I recognize it after a moment -- bondage shorts. Once locked into this thing you're not getting out without the key.

"What's that?" Fischer asks from behind me. There's genuine surprise in his voice.

"A little insurance," Stephens says.

I see where this is going. I accept the shorts and put my legs through the openings.

Fischer approaches to get a closer look. "Hey, wait a minute!" he says to Stephens.

"What?" There's mock innocence in his voice.

"Well, you're leaving the key for that thing, right?"

Stephens pretends to consider. "I wasn't planning on it. Should I?"

I've got the shorts on by this point. Stephens reaches over and starts adjusting the belts.

"Well," Fischer sounds defensive. "I had some, you know, I had some shit planned."

"Like what?" Stephens cinches the waist belt tightly, locks it with a small padlock. Looking down, I notice that my abs are tighter and more defined than I've ever seen them. I hadn't expected that.

Fischer is stopped short, his mouth working soundlessly. Finally he just shakes his head. "Ahhh, the hell with it!" He storms from the room.

Stephens chuckles as he locks the final belt around my thigh. "Heh, heh. I'd say that was pretty damn funny, wouldn't you boy?"

"Sir! Yes, Sir!" I can't resist a smile myself.

Finished with the shorts, Stephens takes a step back to survey them. He plants his gloved hands on his duty belt and nods at me, approvingly. "Looking good, boy. I'd say your special diet and exercise program are paying off." I feel an intense rush of pride, and can't help but look down at the floor. "Thank you, Sir."

He steps toward me, touches the underside of my chin and lifts it. He stares into my eyes for several seconds. "I'll make a good boy of you yet, Fuckhole."

"Thank you, Sir. I'm trying, Sir."

"You're doing good, boy. Just keep it up."

"Yes, Sir."

He leans in for a kiss then, opens his mouth and closes his eyes. I do the same. Our lips meet and his tongue penetrates me. His smell is incredible -- aftershave, coffee, leather and testosterone. In inhale. My tender nipples rub against the front of his uniform, the pressed fabric, the cold metal badge. My dick swells against the hard barrier of the bondage shorts. The frustration is delicious. Officer Stephens grasps my head with both hands, the tight glove leather against my cheeks and temples, and increases the force of his kiss. He presses against me, overpowering me with his mouth and tongue. I dissolve like a lump of sugar, melt against him, hug myself to his hard torso.

Then it ends. Stephens closes his mouth and pulls away. He still holds my head tightly, left hand cradling the back of my skull, right hand on my left cheek. He plunges the leather-clad thumb into my mouth. I suck on it, gazing hungrily into his eyes.

"Damn, boy," he breathes. "You're gonna make me late for work."

I don't answer, just suck on his thumb.

Stephens pulls himself away and half turns toward the door. He increases the pressure on my neck and pushes me ahead of him, grabs my shoulder with the other hand and marches me into the kitchen. Fischer is nowhere to be seen.

"Kneel fucker," Stephens says.

I kneel before the sink. He mixes up another bottle of protein powder -- with tap water instead of piss -- and hands it to me. I drink it down gratefully. Afterward he takes me back to the room with the bondage posts. The gag goes back into my mouth. He fastens and padlocks it around my head. He's got some more gear in there laid out on a chair. He pulls leather mittens over my hands, locks padded restraints around my wrists and locks my wrists to the belt loops of the bondage shorts. He pockets the keys for all this and surveys his work.

"I'll be back late tonight, boy. I suspect you'll be asleep by then. You show Officer Fischer proper respect. You understand?"

I nod.

"Good boy. Back up against that post there."

I do as I am told. Stephens directs his attention to the back of my shorts. I hear the click of a metal snap ring, tethering me to the post. He runs his hands over my bare chest, avoiding the nipples, then leans in close to place his mouth over my ear. I shut my eyes with pleasure.

"You're *my* little fuckhole, aren't you boy?"

"Emmmph phur!" I say, and I mean it.

"Good boy," he says. "Good little fuckhole." And with that Officer Stephens leaves the room, shutting the door behind him.

So I wait. I'm securely attached to the post, with only a little slack to the connection. I can turn from side to side, but it's more comfortable to simply lean back against the face of the post. The thick leather of the waist belt protects the small of my back from the connection hardware. I settle in, close my eyes and downshift into a tranquil frame of mind.

Time passes. I doze. I dream of Patti Hearst with the automatic rifle, see the grainy image captured on the bank security camera. Except something is odd about her face, something not right beneath the dark glasses. It takes me forever to figure it out.

That's not Tanya. That's me.

The door to the room opens and I snap awake. The sunlight has changed. It must be late afternoon. Fischer is entering. He's still shirtless, and he's got a lit cigar stuck in his mouth. He moves to stand a few feet from me and takes a long pull on the cigar. I watch the cherry red coal entombed within gray ash, then he removes it from his mouth and blows smoke in my face. I turn my head, my eyes stinging. I try to hold my breath, but when I do finally breathe the cloud of smoke is still there. I cough around the gag.

Fischer chuckles, cigar back in his teeth. He plants his arms across his thick chest and looks at me squarely. "Well, well, well. Seems your master didn't want me to have a crack at that pretty ass or mouth of yours, huh?"

I stare at him. He's so fucking hot, I almost wish Officer Stephens hadn't protected me. Almost.

"Well, I know a thing or two, boy, don't you worry. I can still have some fun with a piece of meat like you. All I need is to get a little more. . . creative."

I don't even want to think about what that means.

Fischer brushes his fingers across my tender nipples. I flinch, and this causes his grin to widen. "What's wrong there, boy? Your poor little nips sensitive?" He rubs harder, and I groan around the gag. He takes them between thumb and fore-finger and pulls, forcing a wince out of me. I want to wrench myself to the side to dislodge his grip but I know that will only make things worse. Instead I concentrate on breathing, keep my eyes focussed on his, keep my grunts to a minimum. I'm Officer Stephens' boy. I can take whatever this meathead dishes out.

Fischer squeezes and pulls on my nips now as if he expects them to produce milk. Fuck you, Sir! I want to shout. This gag is protecting me in more ways than one.

"Yeah, fucker. Stephens didn't lock up your nipples, now, did he? He leans in close until the cigar's ember is only an inch from my face. I keep my eyes forward, suffer through the smoke. It distracts me from the fire in my nipples. "I'm gonna take a fuckin' cheese grater to these things if you're not careful."

Fischer takes the cigar out of his mouth and then covers my left nipple with his lips. He sucks, runs his tongue over the nipple, and a wave of pain and pleasure ripples outward. It's like a fucking firecracker going off on my chest. I break, whimper, try to protect my nipples. Fischer pushes my shoulders back and goes at my nipple with renewed vigor, decides to work on the other one for a while. The sensation sets me off all over again.

He finally relents and steps backward, laughing. I bend forward at the waist to protect my chest, flex my hands within the mittens, pull on the restraints. If I could only get free I'd wipe that damned smirk off his face!

He takes another pull on the cigar and blows smoke toward the ceiling. He pushes me back against the post until my torso is upright. "Stay, fucker," he commands.

I do, shooting him a nasty look.

Fischer slaps my abs with the back of his hand. He slaps them again, and again, and again, each time harder than the last. I tense up. He smacks again and when I look down, I see a red impression left by the back of his fingers.

"You got more coming, boy."

Fischer makes a fist and pounds my stomach with the fleshy part of his hand. Again. And again. Each impact is harder, though he gives me some time to recover between them. I try to remain rigid, keep my abs rock hard. After a particularly long pause Fischer punches me again, this time with the knuckles. The impact forces me against the post and I spend a moment defenseless and breathing hard.

"Prepare yourself, boy!"

I tense my abs a moment before his fist hits home. I'm better prepared for this one, leaning into it, my feet planted to the rear. He pulls back and punches me with his right fist, then his left, then his right again. I stand there with granite abs and I take it. I fucking take it.

WHAM!

Fuck you, Sir!

WHAM!

Fuck you, Sir!

WHAM!

Is that all you fuckin' got, Sir?

Fischer takes the cigar out of his mouth. He's breathing hard now as he looks me up and down. I'm leaning toward him, chin up and chest out proud, breathing heavily as well. I stare into his eyes and don't look away.

He simply nods and returns the cigar to his mouth.

Fischer unlatches me from the post and guides me into another room. This one's got a battered couch and an old TV in it. He indicates a spot on the floor in front of the couch for me to sit. I do. He switches on the TV, finds a baseball game in progress, leaves the room for a moment and comes back with a cold beer. He plants himself on the sofa to watch the game.

I watch with him. I haven't much choice, tied up and gagged the way I am. I've never had any interest in baseball, and though I understand the rules I can't muster any enthusiasm for it. Some of the players are hot, though. Is Mark Maguire still playing? Damn, he was woofy. I slip back into an easy-going state of mind. The shorts and gag are comfortable, though my hands are sweating inside these mittens. Taking a piss might be a problem but if I need to do that I'm confident I'll handle it when the situation arises.

The room goes dark as the sunlight fades outside. Fischer watches the game silently, finishes his beer and gets another. I occasionally risk glances toward him. His eyelids are drooping, his mouth just a little slack in the blue glow from the television. That's right, I think. Take a nap. I won't mind. Could I get out of the house even in this get up? Maybe. I could take off down the road and have a full night to find other people. It would be risky, but then, so would be waiting around for these two to get bored with me.

The baseball game ends. Fischer gets a third beer from the kitchen and pops a DVD into the player atop the TV. He plants himself back on the couch as the movie starts. It's a porno. There are two guys on a ship, one a master in full leather and the other a young crackerjack. The master is working over the crackerjack, gets him naked, shoves a monster dildo up his ass and pisses on him. They're both very handsome, and the action is hot so it isn't long before I've got an erection inside the shorts. I shift position, forcing my stiff dick against the stiffer leather.

The room is suddenly flooded with yellow light. I look over to see Fischer lighting a fresh cigar. He gets it going, takes a long pull and blows smoke toward the ceiling. I see he's got his dick out as well, the waistband of his sweat pants pulled down. The head of his dick reaches all the way to the dark and flattened navel of his furry gut. Fischer's dick looks so tasty.

There's yelping from the TV. I look over and see that the leather master has the crackerjack chained to the ceiling now, and he's whipping his ass bright cherry. I whimper through the gag and feel my dick spit out some precum. Damn, I'd loved to be worked over like that! Fischer doesn't notice. Instead he squirts some lube onto his dick and begins stroking it. He's in no hurry. I inhale deeply in order to pick up the scent of his cigar. The action continues on screen. The leather master just keeps working over the boy. Damn -- I've got to get this movie! My dick is straining inside the shorts.

The porno moves on to an orgy scene with new actors. There's more bondage and fucking in this one. Fischer is pumping his cock faster now, the cigar still clenched in his teeth, and the springs of the couch are groaning under his weight. I suddenly feel a flash of anger. Abducting me, raping me, forcing me to drink their piss -- that's one thing. But making me watch this movie and not letting me jerk-off -- now that's over the line!

"Fuck this!" Fischer says suddenly. He stands up, places himself in front of me, kicks my legs together to give himself a comfortable place to stand. I look up, helpless. He's a hulking dark shape blocking the TV, silhouetted in the blue glow, his eyes invisible but the tip of the cigar bright red. He's pumping his cock, his shoulders convulsing, smoke pouring from his mouth like a Chinese dragon. I can still hear the audio from the movie, grunts and whimpers and porn-movie encouragement.

"Yeah, fuck me!"

"Yeah, you take that!"

Fischer towers over me and jerks himself off. He's slapping his chest now, gobs of sweat raining down from above.

He's grunting. I can't tell which noises are coming from him and which are from the TV. The cigar glows and fades, glows and fades, and I whimper. I want to lick his balls, to lift my legs and feel his cock ream my ass but none of that is possible. I whimper again, louder this time, more from frustration than anything else.

"Yeah, fuckhole. You take that cock!"

That was Fischer -- I think. I grunt as if I'm getting fucked. "Emmmph phur. . ."

"Yeahhhh. . ." I love to hear him talk around the cigar. His voice deep, so fucking sexy. I still can't see his face but I imagine he's got his eyes closed.

I whimper loud and pained through the gag. I keep it up, pull at the restraints so that they make noise as well. Fischer is convulsing above me, grunting out commands for me to take his cock. The porn actors on the TV egg him on.

"FFFFuuuuuuuuuuuuuuuck!" The sound is ripped from Fischer's throat and at that moment I'm showered with cum. It splashes onto my chest like hot wax, thick and heavy, onto my face, my head, my shoulder. His cum hits my belly, my face again. Is it all cum? Is it sweat? It smells salty and yeasty like bread dough, slides down my chest, drips onto my forearm.

Someone has come on the screen as well.

Simultaneous orgasm.

I stare up at Fischer, aware of my own raging hard on. My balls are definitely going to hurt in a little while. Fischer takes the cigar out of his mouth and stands there for several moments, breathing hard. The actors on the movie are still at it, fucking as if nothing has happened, and that breaks the spell. Fischer continues to stand there, stretches his neck, pulls up the waistband of his pants. His cum has gone runny now, dripping down my forehead and onto my cheek.

"Jesus," Fischer says, "you're a fucking mess."

He walks over to the table beside the couch, stubs out his cigar and turns on the lamp. Weak yellow light floods the room. On the porn movie someone's squatting on a cock. Fischer hits the remote and the TV shuts off. He walks back over to me, plants his hands under my arm pits and hoists me up. I stand in front of him, still restrained, dwarfed by his bulk. The smell of cum and sweat and tobacco is strong in my nose.

He takes me by my left tricep. "All right, Fuckhole, gotta get you cleaned up. Wouldn't want your precious Officer Stephens to see you like this, now, would we?"

No, I don't suppose so. Fischer leads me through the darkened house, not to the enema room like I expect but to the back door. He unlocks it and takes me outside. The night air is cool against my wet chest and face. He marches me down the steps and orders me to kneel on the hard-packed ground. I do. He stands two paces in front of me, reaches into his sweatpants and removes his softening cock, points it at me. He labors to start a stream of piss after his orgasm. Judging by his grimace it's taking a lot of effort. He does finally start to piddle on the ground. He breathes hard, lets loose a grunt and then the stream intensifies, crosses the gulf between us and splashes on my stomach. It falters but then comes back stronger and now he's showering me with it. I close my eyes and bow my head, feel the stream trace lazy arcs across my body.

"Yeeeaaaaaahhhhhhhhh," Fischer groans.

He hoses down my head, chest, abs and arms. The stream is warm but has almost no smell -- beer piss. I feel it pool around the waistband of the bondage shorts, work its way inside and dribble down my cock. The piss drips down my back, down my legs and onto the ground where it makes a muddy gruel.

Suddenly it strikes me as a shame, all this piss on the ground. I counted three beers going in but it feels like six coming out, and finally he's done. I look up, see that he's already got his cock back in his pants. He makes a self-satisfied grunt.

"There we go. All nice and clean."

He lifts me by the armpits again and takes me back into the house, back to my bedroom. He orders me to sit on the bed, fastens a padded collar around my neck and attaches me by chain to the bed frame. The piss is drying on my skin, though my hair is still wet. My knees are painted with circles of dark mud.

"Time for night-night, Fuckhole." Fischer pushes me back onto the bed, lifts my legs and positions me in the center. I'm still locked in the shorts and gag, hands restrained to my waist, neck chained to the bed. Once again, I'm not going anywhere.

He shuts off the light and closes the door behind him.

It's a long time before sleep comes to me. Time for my mind to run free the way my body cannot. I think of bank robberies, of being alone in this room.

I think of having a purpose.

I think of being a Fuckhole.

Day Four

I wake the next morning to find Officer Stephens standing beside my bed. The ranch is quiet, the room murky despite early morning sunlight filtering in through the dirty window pane. Stephens is in uniform, minus the Stetson and the sunglasses. The stipple of a twelve-hour beard covers his strong chin. He's gazing intently out the window, as if looking for something he doesn't see. His expression is unguarded. He's almost a different person.

I breathe shallowly, trying not to draw his attention. I want to watch for as long as I can. I'm amazed that he tramped in here and raised the blind without waking me. It seems I now sleep very soundly in bondage gear, chained to a bed and reeking of another man's piss. As I watch, the sunlight sharpens from pink to orange to pale yellow. A yawn overtakes me. I try to suppress it but it's no use, and I shift on the bed. Leather creaks. Chain rattles. My flesh sticks to itself, my hands embryonic within the leather mittens. When I look up again Stephens is watching me. He wrinkles his nose.

"Damn, boy. You stink."

I exhale. This is true.

"Fischer put you to bed wet, I take it. Well, I suppose it coulda been worse."

I nod again.

He returns his attention out the window, searching again. "I had a long shift, boy. Whole time I was out there, all I could think about was coming back here." He pauses, the sound of birds outside filling the gap. "I wanted to get back here to my fuckhole." He turns and rests his gloved fingers on my cheek. The clean smell of the leather cuts through the stink of the piss. He smoked a cigar sometime last night. I can smell it.

"My fuckhole," Officer Stephens says, stroking my cheek. "My little fuckhole. . ."

I close my eyes and enjoy the feeling, the warmth of his attention.

He sighs. "All right, boy. We've got a lot of work to do today, but first we got to get you cleaned up."

I realize with a start that it's Sunday. These men have been holding me since Thursday, and today is the party, the whole reason for my abduction. Then what? What happens when they no longer need me? I shouldn't think about it -- it will only cloud my mind. In the confusion later there should be a chance for me to get away. I've just got to stay alert.

Stephens peels me out of the bondage gear, careful not to soil himself. The feel of the cold air on my crotch and hands is amazing, turns my body to gooseflesh. He orders me to stand before him. He shackles my wrists in front of me with the hand-cuffs taken from his duty belt, then turns and walks for the door. "Follow me," he says without glancing behind. I do. There's no sign of Fischer as he takes me across the hall to the white-tiled enema room. He locks the door behind us, pocketing the key, and then quietly undresses. The gloves come first, followed by the duty belt and boots. I would help if he gave the merest signal, but instead he loosens his pants and removes his shirt, shows me that beautiful chest and six pack. I stand by, not leering but not wanting to miss a moment of the show. Presently he stands there naked, tall and strong. He points to the shower off in the corner. "Over there, boy."

He has me stand under the shower head, pushes my arms up over the fixture, trapping me. I have to stand on tip-toes to get my wrists over the shower head, but once on the other side and against the wall it's not that much of a stretch. The tile is cold against my back and ass. Stephens starts the water. It's ice cold as it hits my legs but I can bear it. He adds hot water. "You tell me when it's comfortable, boy." Before long it is, and I nod to him. He enters the stall. Hot water splashes off his deltoids and traps, his eyes closed as he stretches and lets it stream down his body. The water spray hits my eyes, making it difficult to keep them open, but I watch as best I can.

He takes a bar of soap and lathers up. I watch him scrub his scalp, his pecs and abs, lather drifting down and off his cock. He soaps himself thoroughly then rinses off, looks me in the face. I stare into his eyes, waiting for instruction.

He lifts his right arm, presses the pit into my face. "Lick it, fuckhole. Lick it clean."

Without hesitation I lap at his arm pit. My tongue parches from a trace of antiperspirant, his hair tickling my nose, but I don't let that stop me. I dig in. Stephens moans encouragement, leans into my tongue, and when I'm done with that side we clean the other. He steps back into the water then to finish the job. He redirects the shower stream on me. After I'm drenched head to toe he flicks an overhead lever and the water shuts off. He takes the soap to my skin, scrubbing away the last of Fischer's piss. He soaps up my head, forcing me to shut my eyes, then moves down to my cock.

"Open those legs, boy."

I do, but apparently not to his satisfaction because he kicks my legs out wider, stretching me painfully by my cuffed hands. I'm blind, breathing through my mouth with my head inclined downward. He lathers up my exposed cock, strokes me until I'm fully erect, and then swats at my free-hanging balls. I jerk, desperate to protect my balls but also trying not to cut my wrists overhead. I hear him chuckle. After several minutes of this he orders me to face the wall. I turn, crossing my forearms overhead, and he lathers up my back. He orders me to stick out my ass, and his soapy hands linger there, a finger probing my crack until it plunges in deep. I suck in a breath but don't flinch. I've been trained well. He finger-fucks me, one then two then three fingers. I clench my sphincter around his fingers and wonder if his cock will be next, the idea making my own jump. The soap is irritating. I've never felt more open, more raw or vulnerable. He leans in then, several fingers up my ass, left arm around my soapy chest, and whispers in my ear: "Yeaaaaaah, boy. Get you all nice and clean."

"Yes, Sir," I breathe. "Thank you. . . thank you, Sir."

"Gooooooood boy. Gooooood fuckhole."

After we're both rinsed off, Stephens towels himself dry. He leaves me cuffed and standing by the wall, dripping, while he shaves. When he's done he looks at me thoughtfully for several moments. Is he going to shave me? I keep my eyes down. Apparently he decides against it, calls me over and hands me a fresh disposable razor. He tells me to shave my own face. In the mirror I can see I'm looking scraggly, bags under my eyes and my cheeks sunken from weight loss. Once I'm done he takes me outside again. I can smell coffee brewing. In the kitchen there's a half pot sitting on the warmer. I've never craved anything so much in my life! He sees my gaze, chuckles, and leaves it at that. Instead he pours me some orange juice, and once I've drunk that, mixes up a piss-and-protein shake.

A shoulder and abdominal workout follows, and when we're done, he hoses me down and cleans out my ass again. Fischer wanders to the doorway and looks in, mug of coffee in his hand. His hair is matted from sleep, and I see he's wearing last night's sweatpants.

"Sleeping beauty finally wake up?" Stephens asks.

Fischer grunts.

"Maybe not," Stephens says. "You better make yourself presentable. We only got a couple of hours before things get started."

"Yeah, I'm on it," Fischer says. "Just waiting for you to finish fucking around in here."

"We're done," Stephens says. "Shower's all yours."

Stephens takes me to another bedroom, one I haven't seen so far. There are two metal-framed beds here, a couple of suitcases with dirty clothes tossed about the floor. This must be where they sleep. There's a garment bag hanging on the back of a closet door. Stephens strips off his sweats and pulls on a jock. He instructs me to open the bag, and within it I find a clean uniform with knife-edged creases. I help him dress. Afterward he stands and inspects himself in a full length mirror. I stand by, naked with hands clasped behind my back. I can't help but glance at his reflection. It's such a thrill, being naked in this man's presence. Stephens gives me a jock strap and a pair of work boots I recognize from my luggage. I almost gasp when I see them -- a reminder of my previous life. He picks up a pair of bolt-cutters and a shopping bag from a local hardware store. "Follow me, boy."

He takes me into the pool room, seats himself in the shoeshine chair. He points to the space in front of him. I kneel. He bends forward, places his hand beneath my chin and lifts my head with the slightest touch. I look up into his eyes.

"Today is very important, boy. You understand that, don't you?"

"Yes, Sir."

"Everyone will know that I've trained you. Your behavior will be a reflection on me. Perform well and I will reward you. But if you disappoint me, boy, I swear there'll be hell to pay. You understand?"

"Yes, Sir!"

"Very well." He reaches into the bag and pulls out a short length of steel chain. He drapes it around my neck, checking for length, trims it with the bolt cutters and tests it again. Satisfied, he locks the chain in place with a shiny metal padlock. The collar is snug but not uncomfortable, the lock a heavy cold presence atop my breastbone. He holds the lock in his hand for a few moments, considers it, then drops it with a solid *thump* against my chest.

"Okay, boy. Let's get to work."

There's much to do. I'm told we'll have over twenty men here today, each with at least one boy or slave. Fischer and Stephens' room will be locked, but I tidy up in there first, picking up the dirty clothes and stowing the suitcases. Stephens goes ahead of me, room to room, and gives me instructions on each. Fischer heads out for groceries. I've got dishes to wash, ashtrays to empty, floors to sweep and mop. These men are pigs, really, and the work keeps me busy, sweat beading on my naked skin.

Fischer returns with provisions. I cut vegetables, ice drinks and set out snacks. I'm almost done before I think to myself how little I've had to eat. The idea of gobbling any of this food hasn't even occurred to me. I haven't been watched all that closely for the last half hour or so, but it's as if the chain around my neck stands in for Officer Stephens. I want to get rid of it, but then think of how alone I'd feel if I did. I've got to come up with an escape plan! These men won't need me after today, and then what? I imagine that, of all today's attendees, not everyone will be in on their scheme. Someone at the party will help me. I've just got to watch the men and figure out who I can trust. Or maybe there'll be enough confusion that I can slip away myself. The trick will be to stay alert.

My preparations are winding down as the men start to arrive. Every master enters dressed either in leather or uniform. Slaves are naked or nearly so, dragging heavy luggage behind, and when the bags are opened I see they contain enough S&M gear to stock the vendor's room at IML. There are whips, floggers, restraints, chains, paddles and the like. Some of the men arrive in pick-up trucks, and I am dispatched outside with other slaves to carry in paddling benches, sawhorse, portable slings, and even a fuckbench fashioned from welded steel and rubber padding. Stephens and Fischer socialize with the masters, ignore the slave boys. Everyone seems to know one another. The slaves are silent except when answering questions put to them by the topmen. When I have a chance I try to make eye contact with the slaves but it's no use. They're trained as well as Bobby was. I am put on various details, hanging slings, assembling a St. Andrews cross, sorting through restraints and coil after coil of rope. I've lost track of Officer Stephens but there's always my collar, not to mention at least one master supervising. I don't know yet whom to trust, so I keep my mouth shut and concentrate on the work.

Eventually the preparations are over and the party gets underway. This happens gradually. I go past one of the rooms and see three boys tied up, two being tortured and one just left to watch. The lighting in the sling room has been dimmed, chains rattling inside. Stephens, carrying a clipboard, finds me and orders me to follow him to the front room, to where Fischer kept me tied up last night. The TV is playing pornos again with the sound turned low, the moaning on the video matching that from the rest of the ranch. A simple wooden chair and folding table has been placed by the door. Stephens attaches a leash to my chain and orders me to kneel by the chair. I do, and he seats himself. Next to me is a grimy window that looks out on the front yard. An SUV has just parked, and the driver -- an African-American man in a CHP uniform -- is directing his lanky boy to gather up some luggage. The CHP waits for a pick-up truck to park, and when it does, he warmly greets the driver. I watch this slyly, keeping my gaze mostly downward. The masters approach the front door with their subs trailing behind. They enter and greet Stephens without glancing at me.

"Hey, bud!" the black CHP says. His perfectly detailed uniform hugs his tall frame like a second skin. "How you been?"

"I've been just great, Mark. Hey there, Phil," Stephens says to the other top. This man is in his sixties, I'd guess, and dressed in loose-fitting chaps and harness. "Excellent to see you both. You come in from Atlanta?"

"Yeah, yesterday," Phil says. "Stayed at some fleabag down the road."

"I know the place. I'll need to see your invitations before I can let you in."

"Certainly," Phil says. He snaps his fingers. "Front and center, boy!" Phil's boy duck-waddles to stand before the card table. He's a compact slab of muscle just a bit younger than his Sir, freshly shaven head, powdery-white horseshoe moustache and mouth stretched wide around a pink rubber ball gag. He turns around for inspection and I see his wrists are tied behind his back, a pronounced hump between his shoulders betraying a long history with anti-viral drugs. He's wearing tight red latex posing trunks with the word "CUB" printed across the ass. He bends forward, and his Sir scrunches the trunks downward, revealing an asshole stuffed with a fat black butt plug. That explains the duck-waddle. Painted in white on the bottom of the plug is a circle about two inches in diameter, a single star inscribed within.

Stephens nods his approval. "Damn good. Would love to score some time with that ass a bit later."

Phil pulls up the latex trunks. "Sure," he says. "Just come see me when you're ready."

"Will do. How about you, Mark?"

"Got it right here," Mark says. He pushes his boy forward and turns him around. The loose skin of his right butt cheek has been cut with something sharp, the scab forming the same design as Phil's boy had. "We did it a little different this year."

"May I?" Stephens asks.

"By all means," Mark says. "Bend over, faggot."

'Faggot' bends over, and Stephens reaches out to probe the scarring with his gloved hand. He traces the lines.

"Nice work."

Mark nods. "Thanks. Of course, he hollered a bit when I did it, so we had to spread the work out over several sessions, but I think it was worth it."

"I agree," Stephens says. He marks their names off on his list. "You gentlemen have a great time. I'll be in to chat later."

This process repeats itself several times over the next hour. Each sub comes in with the same symbol either cut, tattooed, burned, or simply marked in pen on the ass, usually the right cheek. This except for one boy so heavily tattooed there is no room on his ass or any other piece of skin for the symbol. Stephens knows this couple well and doesn't bother to ask for the invitation. Men drift in and out of the room, talking, snacking or watching the porn. Most already know each other, though some are introduced for the first time. The relationships between dom and sub fall along a spectrum from loose to formal. Some of these men call their boys by their first names and involve them in conversation, while others refer to their subs as "it" and treat them accordingly. Regardless, none of these subs appears to be a prisoner of the man who holds him. If I just start pleading for help right now, could I bring this whole ordeal to an end?

I keep silent. It's best if I wait.

Time passes. My knees ache from kneeling. In fact, I realize they've been aching for a while but I've ignored the pain. A tall, beefy man with reddish-brown hair and goatee approaches. He's dressed in leather breeches, Dehner patrol boots and chest harness, a fat piece of anodized steel piercing his left nipple. A naked, shaven-headed slave walks behind him on a leash. Stephens stands as the man approaches and they chat for a bit as he takes over the chair and clipboard. Stephens bids him a good day and then tugs on my leash, leading me from the room. We wander, Stephens in the lead with me a respectful few paces behind. Men are playing pool, their slaves tied up or kneeling around the perimeter of the room. Watersports are happening in the tiled room, wax play also. The loudest moaning seems to be coming from the room with all the slings. We enter. It's dark in there, hot and airless, the only light coming from red bulbs in portable work lights clamped to the rafters.

I see Fischer. He's in uniform, his shirtsleeves rolled up to the elbows and his right fist buried in the greasy asshole of some hooded boy. Stephens stands off to the side for a good view, and I look over his shoulder. The boy's hands are restrained, his boots lashed to the sling's chains. Fischer pulls his arm back, pushes it forward, rocking the boy to and fro. Fischer's head is wreathed in smoke, the cherry glow of his cigar matching the glint of the lights overhead. Stephens reaches down and massages the front of his pants. He turns to me. "You ever have that asshole of yours opened up with a fist, boy?" His voice is low, either tender or menacing I can't tell.

I shake my head from side to side. I'm way too tight for that stuff. "No, sir."

He nods. "I didn't think so. Still, there's a time and place for everything."

I cast my eyes downward, thinking it unwise to plead with him. I've endured much this weekend. Could I take a fist?

We watch Fischer work the boy over a while longer. The boy is moaning loudly but his dick is as soft as fresh ice cream. Men come and go, and further back in the room someone screams as an orgasm rips him apart. Fischer crushes his cigar underfoot, bends over to gnaw on the boy's nipples all the while keeping his fist firmly planted. The boy's cock jerks and spits pre-cum but stays soft.

"Damn!" Stephens hisses. "I've got to get me some of that!" He looks back at me. "Come on, Fuckhole!"

I don't dare disobey, but I'm sure my eyes show my terror. He takes me to an empty sling and orders me into it. I climb in and lift my legs, notice my hands are trembling as I hold the chains. He attaches my wrists overhead, puts my feet through soft leather straps. He disappears for a moment, returns with a piss gag which he shoves into my mouth and latches behind my head. He adjusts me in the sling until my ass is out further, cantilevered over the far edge. I see him take a marker from his pocket. He uncaps it, the scent of alcohol strong in my nose, and writes something on my ass. The marker leaves a cold wet trail against my skin, a few words written on either side of my hole. He inspects his work and then smiles at me.

"You hang out here, boy. I'll be back for you."

With that he turns and leaves the room. I watch him go, feeling alone and very, very vulnerable. The sling is comfortable, and he's tied me in such a way that I'm not constricted or stretched. The padlock around my neck feels like a warm heavy paper weight. The moist heat of the room soothes like a wool blanket, the red glow like sunlight filtered through closed eyelids. I could almost fall asleep, yet I'm keenly aware of my asshole hanging exposed in close proximity to latex gloves and Elbow Grease. What did Stephens write on my ass? A warning? An invitation?

Another sling hangs just a few feet to my right. The couple using it are oblivious to anyone but themselves, the heat of their love-making eclipsing that of the room. The bottom's back is arched, his face contorted in silent ecstasy, the top leaning in almost close enough to kiss. Fisters always seem so. . . transported by what they do. Maybe if Stephens were to fist me

I would enjoy it. I don't know. I'm afraid.

Just then I see him return to the room. He's got that older boy in tow, the fireplug with the latex posing trunks, naked now and free of the butt plug. Stephens helps him up into an empty sling. The boy spreads his legs wide while Stephens pulls on a pair of gloves. I watch, relieved yet disappointed. Their action is slow and insular, and eventually, I grow sleepy and stare at the ceiling.

Time slips on. Moaning fills the room, dies away. Some men inspect me as they walk by, read the message written on my ass. I try not to meet their eyes but my dick grows under their attention. I like hanging here, on display. Some men rub my cock or pinch my nipples, but no one makes to fist me. I hang for an hour, probably longer. Officer Stephens has left the room. I doze.

I'm aware of someone approaching. I see him through the V-shaped frame of my legs. It's the tall, muscular master with the reddish goatee who relieved Stephens at the check-in desk, the one with the fat steel through his left nip. Behind him I see the demure shape of his sub. The top looks at my ass a moment, runs his hands up and down my legs, fixes me with his stare. "Get me a glove and some lube," he says, apparently to his boy. "Yes, sir," the boy says quickly and darts away. He returns a moment later.

The man frees my cock and balls from the jock pouch, closes his hand around my balls and tugs firmly. The pressure feels good. I swing toward him, and then he pushes and I swing back. He increases the energy until I'm swaying forward and back. It feels strange but also good. He lets me swing freely while he dons the rubber glove, pours a stream of lube into the palm and coats his fingers. He lubes up my ass, carefully stud-ies my eyes while he probes me with one finger, in and out, then a second finger, a third. I wriggle in the sling, trying to raise my ass toward him, to make myself accessible. His boy stands by, eyes down. The man pushes but stays at three fingers. There was a time when three fingers would have been difficult for me to take, but after the pounding I've received this weekend my ass opens easily. I moan through the piss gag as this man skillfully probes my hole, massages the prostate and the hard knot of bone behind my rectum. My dick swells.

He looks back at his boy and points at my cock. "Go to work on that, boy."

"Sir! Yes, Sir!" The boy moves to the side of the sling, bends down and takes my cock in his mouth. Every neuron of my brain fires then, the combination of this man's fingers and his boy's mouth are electric. I moan loudly, wriggle and buck. God, this is incredible!

The man smiles as he works my ass. He swings me erratically, side to side, forward and back. Occasionally the boy fails to match the movement, and my cock slips from his mouth. When this happens the man swats him hard on the ass, orders him to do a better job. My nuts boil but I get nowhere near climax. Eventually the top gets bored of this and orders his boy to bend over my mid-section, ab to ab. He takes down a paddle from the wall and beats the boy's ass until he's crying, his entire body shuddering atop me.

The master holds his weeping boy against his chest, soothing him. I am forgotten. They wander away, my mid-section cold without the boy covering it. I wait. Stephens returns. His sleeves are rolled up to the elbows but the fireplug seems to have been returned to his master. "You have a good time, boy?"

"Gaaahhhh," I say.

He pats my ass, my stomach, pinches my nipples. He lays his hand across my face and inserts several fingers through the piss gag. I taste a hint of soap on his fingers. "Yeah," he says. "I can see you've had some fun. I've got some other plans for you though. Come on."

He frees me and helps me down to the floor. It takes me a moment to get my footing, but once I do, he orders me to stuff my cock back into the jock pouch. Then he secures my hands behind my back and connects my ankles with a short length of chain. He marches me from the room, the piss gag still in my mouth, and leads me to where a poker game is in progress. This room is crowded by a round table too large for the space, cards, chips and ashtrays strewn across the green felt top. Cigar smoke overwhelms me, thick and strong as if all the air in the room has been displaced. A fluorescent light fixture in a green glass shade barely punches through the smoke, casting everything in the sickly glow of a Vegas casino at three in the morning.

I count four men playing cards, an empty chair available for a fifth. Against the far wall are three slaves restrained with hands behind backs, ankles chained, piss gags in faces. Above them is a computer-printed banner that reads: URINALS. Stephens takes me to this wall and chains my bound hands to a waist-high latch. He holds my face and looks into my eyes, slaps my cheek. "Yeah, fucker. You be good while I steal money from these poor bastards."

I nod silently.

He moves toward the open chair and greets the other players. One of them in particular stands out. He's a burly guy, thicker than he is tall with a neck the size of my thigh. His hair is mostly blonde but with some red mixed in, medium cut with a bushy moustache and clean-shaven chin. He's not wearing leather or a uniform but rather a white dress shirt with vintage styling, suspenders and a necktie. He's got that chest-holster plainclothes detectives on TV wear, gun stowed near his left pec.

Stephens greets him enthusiastically, a manner that seems a bit forced. "Detective Swint! I thought I might find you in here."

Swint smiles around the cigar in his mouth. "Having a friendly game." Another player grunts unhappily.

Stephens seats himself and lights up a cigar, adding to the haze of the room. A naked slave stands at attention in the opposite corner. Stephens calls for a beer, and the slave quickly slips from the room. He returns a moment later, kneels with head bowed beside Stephens and offers up the beer. I glance to my left where the other urinal slaves are chained. Each stands more or less at attention, eyes forward, chest out proudly. After a moment, one of the players gets up to relieve himself. Unzipping his pants, he squeezes around the table to the slave on the far end. The slave kneels, lifting his head to present the opening of the gag. The man pisses down the slave's throat, the slave's Adams apple bobbing as he takes the load.

The game continues. My eyes water from the cigar smoke. I wish I could rub them but that's not possible. I take two loads of watery beer piss, one from Officer Stephens and one from a cowboy who's busy losing all his money to Detective Swint. Swint appears to be a card shark. The stack of chips in front of him is definitely the largest on the table, and watching him play is like watching one of those nature documentaries on TV where you see a lion take down a gazelle in slow motion. It's an ugly process. Finally, the cowboy decides to exit with some of his dignity intact. He stubs out his cigar, wishes the players a good day and unchains his boy from the wall. About fifteen minutes later Officer Fischer wanders in. Our eyes lock. I quickly look away, but not before I see a nasty grin spread across his face.

"Deal me in, Gentlemen," he says, and orders a beer. Before he takes the empty seat, however, he saunters over and stands in front of me. He touches his zipper, and I obediently lower myself, inclining my head upward toward his fly. I look up into his face, shadowed by the Stetson. Damn, he's hot! His piss starts filling my mouth a moment later, weak and not unpleasant. Afterward he takes his seat. He lights his own cigar and puts on his black aviator sunglasses. I watch cloud formations dance above the table, weather fronts with defined boundaries. I feel light-headed.

"I need some fresh air," says one of the players, although it looks to me he simply wants to stop the hemorrhaging of his chips. He thanks the players and exits, taking another of the urinal slaves with him. That leaves two of us. My shoulders hurt from keeping my hands behind my back, my legs from standing. At least Stephens left me a jock strap -- the other urinal doesn't even have that.

Detective Swint knows what he's doing and he's good at it. I suspect the other men are here for the social aspect, playing poker while their slaves are tied up nearby, but Detective Swint likes to win. This is his way of topping the other tops, humiliating them while their subs look on. He's all business, puffs on his cigar only enough to keep it lit, barely touches the glass of whiskey before him. He seems to focus on one opponent at a time, and now that two others have bowed out he's concentrating on Officer Stephens. Stephens can't bear up. He's getting agitated, sweating, his hand tapping nervously on the table. Doesn't he realize what's going on? He must have seen Swint do this before. No, I'm sure he realizes it. But he's too emotionally invested to stop. There's some history here, something between these two men. Stephens badly wants to win, and in the earlier hands Swint was giving him some ground, but now that's all over. I can watch it all unfold but I can't do anything to stop it. Stephens' stack of chips has been diminishing, and I imagine that soon he'll be forced out of the game. Will he be in a bad mood then? He hasn't beat me out of anger the way Fischer has, but I've never seen him. . . vulnerable like this.

A new hand is dealt, and Detective Swint takes the opportunity to pull long and hard on his cigar, blowing a cloud of smoke in Stephens' direction. It's blatant and provocative, but Stephens has his attention riveted on the cards arriving in front of him. He has opened his shirt collar, and I can see sweat stains spreading out from his underarms.

The players take up their hands. I concentrate on Swint but I can't see what he's holding. He's too large, the cards hidden behind his starched shirt, which I notice is pristine and without a drop of sweat. They ante up. Swint has the first bet. He counts out several chips and puts them in the pot.

Fischer and Stephens exchange glances. I can see part of Fischer's hand and it doesn't look like much, only a pair of queens. He matches the detective's bet anyway. Stephens matches as well, even though he needs to put together a large number of low-value chips to do so.

I glance to the side. The remaining urinal is watching me. Does he belong to Swint? He quickly looks away.

The dealer folds. Swint, Stephens and Fischer take new cards, Fischer three, Stephens and Swint one each. Swint takes a long pull on his cigar, down nearly to the ring now, and stubs out the remainder. He counts several new chips and throws them into the pot. Stephens exhales, while Fischer stares stonily forward. Fischer re-arranges the cards in his hand. I see the same pair of queens and a ten. He considers a bit, then puts the required chips in the pot. "I'm in."

Stephens stares at Detective Swint. "You know I can't match that," he says.

Swint shrugs. "Guess that means you got to fold, partner."

Stephens bites his lip. "Maybe," he says. He rearranges his cards, then looks at me. He jerks his head in my direction. "What about fuckhole over there?"

Swint stares at Stephens. "What about him?"

"I'll put his ass in the pot."

Swint shakes his head. "I already got a slave, buddy. I'm not in the market for another."

Stephens balks. "I'm not selling him -- I'm renting. One hour alone with him. Work him however you want."

"One hour? How do I know he's worth that much?"

"Oh," Fischer says quickly, "he's worth it. I'm fine with having Fuckhole in the pot."

I try to catch Stephen's eye but it's no use. Will he really do this?

Detective Swint looks in my direction, rubs his chin. He stands and comes toward me. I cast my eyes downward. If he refuses, then Stephens has to fold and I'm in no danger. If he agrees. . . Shit, I don't like this.

But an hour with him, alone? Would he help me?

Swint reaches out for my nipples, pulls on them. I wince and lift my head. He increases the pressure, forcing me to grunt through the piss gag, all the while watching Stephens' reaction. "Two hours," Swint says.

"Ninety minutes," Stephens counters.

The detective considers a moment. "Okay. You're on."

Fuck.

He returns to his cards, and Stephens takes a dry napkin. I see him write FUCKHOLE in block letters on it and place it in the pot. "All right, buddy. Let's see 'em."

Detective Swint lays down his cards. "Three aces," he says. They hit the table one by one: spades, hearts, diamonds.

"Damn!" Fischer says. "Two pair!" He throws his cards down.

All eyes turn to Stephens. He's sitting there with a stoic expression, staring at Swint.

"Well?" the dealer asks.

Stephens grimaces and lays down his cards. "Three kings," he says, "you son of a bitch. "

Swint chuckles as he collects the pot. He holds up the napkin. "Well, well, well, what do we have here? Looks like I've won myself a piece of ass."

"Yeah, well," Stephens says. "The clock is ticking, buddy. Hour and a half."

Swint nods. "That's agreeable. I was fixin' to quit anyway." He takes his chips to the drink-runner and cashes out.

Stephens collects the cards and begins shuffling them, even though it's not his deal. He doesn't look in my direction. Swint takes a leash from his pocket and attaches it to the collar of the other urinal. He unlatches him, stands him in front of me facing away, and attaches my collar to his with a short length of chain. He takes a knife from his pocket and cuts the jockstrap from around my waist. My dick swings free, semi-hard. "I like 'em naked," he says.

"Eighty-nine minutes by my watch," Stephens says sourly.

Swint looks at me and grins. "Some folks are just sore losers."

I cast my eyes downward.

Swint makes for the exit. His slave follows, as do I a half-step later. We're both hobbled by the ankle chains, so walking is awkward, but the detective simply walks at a normal pace. I make a quick glance back toward Officer Stephens. He's looking after me and our eyes lock, but then the tension on my chain pulls me from the room.

Detective Swint parades us around the ranch house, through the wet room and the bondage room. In here someone is hanging upside down from the rafters, crying out as the soles of his feet are beaten. In the gym a couple of drill instructors are forcing naked recruits through what looks to be a monster workout, shouted commands bouncing off the hard walls. Swint takes us to the back yard where I'm surprised to see that it's late afternoon. Men are sitting with their boots propped up on their slaves. One sub is getting flogged viciously, gasping for air with his back ruby red.

Swint stops to socialize, taking a seat at the picnic table. Without command his slave goes down on all fours, and I've no choice but to follow, my neck linked to his. The detective places his feet -- I see he's wearing wingtips -- upon his slave's back and lights a fresh cigar.

We wait there while Swint shoots the breeze, recounting the tale of winning me in the card game. Several tops drift toward us and stand around to hear. I can only see their boots. One of them asks if Swint had seen the writing on my ass. He stands up to take a look, and then they all have a good laugh. What the hell does it say? My blood boils. I want to defend Officer Stephens but I can't. The piss gag stops me, but also the chain and padlock around my neck. My behavior reflects on him, so silent obedience is probably the best course here.

After a beer, Swint excuses himself. He stands and tugs on his slave's neck chain. I follow back inside in the wake of his cigar smoke. I've got this chained-ankle-walk down, hands fastened behind my back, tongue papery dry and dick still half-swollen from the poker game. My ass feels empty with nothing inside it but I suppose that will be fixed soon enough. We find our way to Stephens' and Fischer's bedroom. Swint produces a key and unlocks the door. I wonder where he got that. It's dark on the other side of the threshold. His cigar glowing in his mouth, Swint frees his slave's hands, mouth and neck.

"Open that blind, boy."

"Yes, Sir!"

The slave moves off while the detective closes and locks the door. He considers me a moment, reaches out and places his hands against my head. His palm seems as large as a tortilla, cold from the beer he drank a moment ago. He shoves a thumb through the gag opening.

"Gu-uuuuh," I say. I've got to get his attention. If he's going to help me, now is the time to try.

Swint ignores me, continues to probe the opening in the gag.

"Uh-uh," I say.

"You hear that?" Swint asks his slave. "Fuckhole here has something to say."

"Yes, Sir," the slave says with modesty. "I heard."

"Fuckhole here doesn't understand that I like my meat submissive and quiet, does he?"

"No, Sir."

"Uhhhhh," I say.

Detective Swint removes his meaty paw and slaps the side of my head, hard. I see stars. "Take the fucking hint, boy." There's menace in his voice. You take the fucking hint, dumbass! But I quiet down.

Swint nods. "That's better." He looks me over, checks his watch. "I'm going to have some fun with you, boy. Not because you're some special piece of meat. Oh no. I'm going to have fun with you because you belong to that poor excuse for a master out there." He pinches my nose shut, strong enough to hurt. I breathe several times through the gag. Swint takes a long drag on the cigar, removes it from his mouth and exhales into the gag opening. I've no choice but to breathe it in, and suddenly I'm wracked with coughing. The fit lasts for several seconds, and when I finally recover I hear Swint chuckling to himself. "That's a damn good cigar, boy. You should appreciate it."

My eyes are watering. A groan is the only response I can make.

The detective turns back to his slave. "Go and get my bag."

"Yes, Sir." The slave moves toward the door, which the detective unlocks and closes behind him. He regards me again and puts downward pressure on my shoulders. I drop to my knees in front of him. Swint opens the fly of his dress pants, pulls out his cock. It's semi-hard, big-veined and uncut with two tremendous balls hanging beneath. He holds it carefully and pulls the foreskin back to reveal the piss slit. I look up into his eyes, hidden behind a troposphere of smoke. The detective puts the head of his cock closer to the gag opening, and a moment later, a trickle of piss falls onto my tongue. It's strong, like tea left to steep too long. The trickle turns into a stream and before long I'm struggling to drink it all down.

There is a respectful knock on the door, and a moment later I see the bare legs of the slave coming back into the room. He's carrying a black leather satchel. The flow of the detective's piss is slowing, until finally he's tapping out the last few drops. He steps back and looks down at me, a satisfied expression on his face. "You've been trained well, boy."

I nod, feeling an intense rush of pride.

He directs my head downward to get access to the gag

buckle at the back of my head. He undoes the gag and tosses it away. It feels wonderful to have it removed from my mouth, freeing my tongue. I look up at him suddenly.

"Sir! Permission to speak, please, Sir?!"

Detective Swint grabs the back of my head with his meaty hand and rams his cock deep into my mouth. "Permission denied, fuckhole."

"Unnnnngghhh!" I gag around his cock, which is already swelling into my throat. I look up but all I can see are the folds of his dress pants, the pressure on the back of my head unrelenting. Breathing is difficult. I feel myself go light-headed again.

"Get out that ball gag, boy," Swint says to his slave.

"Yes, Sir."

The detective pulls out slightly without freeing my mouth, comes back in, out and in, fucking my face. His hand clutches the back of my skull, never giving me a moment's freedom. When he comes all the way in his fleshy balls press against my chin, forcing my mouth open wider. Finally he pulls himself free, and in the moment I inhale a deep and sweet breath, a rubber ball gag is shoved into my mouth. The rubber pushes my teeth up and around. Swint latches it hard behind my head, slapping my skull for good measure.

"That should shut you up."

I want to cry then but I'm just too tired. Instead I look up with pleading eyes, and that seems to satisfy him. He taps cigar ash on the floor and takes a step back.

"Boy," he commands.

"Yes, Sir?" The slave steps forward.

"Help me undress."

"Yes, Sir." First the slave takes the suspenders off each shoulder, leaves them hanging about his waist. Then he carefully removes the detective's necktie, folds it and places it on the nightstand. The gun holster comes off, then the dress shirt is unbuttoned, revealing the detective's thick chest, cross on a gold chain around his neck, nipples the size of half dollars. The slave carefully removes the shirt, folds it reverently and stows it away. All the while Detective Swint keeps his attention on me, cigar in his teeth, slowly massaging his cock. He orders the slave to spend a few moments sucking his nipples, then commands him to suck on his meat. While the slave kneels there and concentrates on his master's cock, and all I can see of him is his shaved head working slowly back and forth, Detective Swint stares at me. I imagine I see a bulge in the back of the slave's throat but I know that can't be. Can it? "Yeah, boy," Swint moans, eyes half closed. "Get it nice and hard."

They continue like this for a while, and then the detective orders his slave to stand. His cock is proud and full now, a blue-veined monster. He's going to kill me with that thing, I just know it. My jaw is aching from the gag but I suspect I'll soon have other things to worry about.

The slave continues undressing his master. The wingtips come off, then the dress pants, everything stowed with the same degree of care. Finally, Swint is left standing with just the cigar and black dress socks held up by old-fashioned sock garters. The slave steps back respectfully, and the detective advances on me. "Stand up, fuckhole." I stand slowly. It's difficult with my hands bound, my knees aching, but once up I regard him proudly. We're about the same height, and the fact that we're now both naked, or nearly so, is comforting. But he's the one in control here. There's no mistaking that.

Swint releases my ankles from the chain, turns me around and pushes me toward the bed. "Get your ass over there, faggot. I'm tired of playing with you."

I obey and walk forward. At the bed he pushes me down until my chest is against the mattress, ass up in the air. He kicks my legs out to either side. I support myself with my face and thighs against the mattress. I feel a cold, slick stream of lube kiss my asshole, and I clench myself to make it pucker. Thick, manicured fingers probe me, open my hole, force the lube deep inside. I exhale and open my ass as easy as opening my eyes. There's the sound of a condom package being opened, a pause while the detective protects himself, and then I'm feeling the head of his meat against my hole. I have a moment's terror, thinking it's just too big, but then the pressure is like an old friend and suddenly I know I can take it. I bear down, open my hole, and take Detective Swint deep into my gut.

"Uhhhh, yeah fuckhole. Goooood job. . ." he says. I smell the cigar smoke intensely then, see it pool around the bed, feel his weight on top of me, pressing me into the mattress. His skin is cold, his body temperature several degrees lower than it should be. His meaty hands grip my shoulders and he drives himself into my ass. I open wide to accommodate him, give him everything I have. My legs curl backward, my head rears and I bite down on the ball gag.

Oh, fuck me, Sir, I think. Fuck me like the piece of meat I am.

He does, settling in for a nice sloppy time. My hole numbs up, the only way I know he's home is when his balls slap against my own. I bear down, savoring muscle soreness left over from this morning's ab workout. I rock with him. I grunt. I buck my ass and massage his fat cock. How could I have ever lived without a cock up my ass? Swint holds me tight, fucks me good. Across the rumpled sheets I see his slave standing with hands clasped behind his back. His cock is proud and full, dripping. I close my eyes and enjoy the sensation of being reamed. Detective Swint keeps working me. He's quiet, businesslike, and despite the heat of the room I feel no sweat drip onto my back. I float in the darkness behind my eyelids, pinned beneath his cock. Suddenly he pulls out, turns me over until I'm on my back, arms trapped beneath me, and lifts up my ankles for his slave to take. I feel even more helpless than before, empty without his cock inside me. The detective regards my hole for a moment, the cigar barely a stub in his mouth. He plays with his nipples and cock.

"Fuck yeah," he says, exhaling smoke. He kneels on the mattress, leans in and fills me up again. I close my eyes. My dick swells, rock hard.

Detective Swint fucks me like he was only playing before, each thrust savage and strong. I see stars every time he comes home. He grunts, the gold cross slapping in the valley between his thick pecs. I want to cry out but the gag prevents me. I want to thank him. I want to bend forward and lick his nipples, suck his slave's cock.

I want to shout with joy. Fuck me! Fuck me! Fuck me!

And then he comes, cross glinting between his pecs, nipples swollen and pink. My sphincter throbs, and it's only as the sensation diminishes over the next few moments that I realize he's injecting me -- or at least the condom between us -- with several pints of cum. His pelvis jitters with tiny convulsions. I feel warmth blossom outward. Detective Swint relaxes slowly, exhales long streamers of smoke from his mouth and nose. He tosses the cigar to the floor behind my head. I hear the boot stamp of his slave putting it out.

The detective relaxes, looks down at me. "Good fuck, boy." He nods with approval. "Good fuck."

Thank you, Sir. I close my eyes and return the nod.

The slave is still obediently holding my ankles. His dick is softening, a stream of pre-cum leaking down my temple and off my ear. I gaze up at him, see his attention riveted on his master. Detective Swint pulls out of my ass, backs himself toward the edge of the bed, stands there with his softening cock weighed down by the load of jizz in the head of the condom. He snaps his fingers, and wordlessly the slave releases my ankles, moves to the other side of the bed and kneels at his master's feet. He gazes up into Detective Swint's eyes, and they stay that way for several seconds, connected by sight. Finally, Swint nods almost imperceptibly, and the slave carefully removes the condom, squeezing the cock as he goes to get every last bit of jizz. He reverently lifts the condom to his lips, eyes closed, and drinks his master's cum. When he's done, Detective Swint pats his shaved head. "Good boy."

The slave rests his head against his master's meaty thigh. "Sir! Thank you, Sir!"

The connection between these men is so big it crowds out everything else in the room. I am left cold and alone on the bed.

Swint blinks and shakes his head, looks down at his watch. "All right, boy, let's get this mess cleaned up."

"Sir, yes Sir!"

By mess, apparently, they mean me. The boy rolls me over and unlatches my hands. I sigh with relief, my shoulders aching from the strain. He ties me spread-eagled on the bed and removes his master's gag. I'm so exhausted from the fuck I don't even think to ask for help. I simply stare, numb. He re-inserts Officer Stephens' piss gag and then attends to his master, helping him dress in what is obviously a much-practiced routine. Afterward, Detective Swint is back in his tie and dress shirt, not a single hair out of place. They are preparing to leave when he casts a last glance back at me. He looks thoughtfully at my cock, then turns to his slave. "Get me a leather cord, boy."

"Sir! Yes Sir!" The boy digs through the leather satchel for a moment and produces a leather cord tied into a neat loop. He hands it to his master.

Swint approaches me with a half smile on his lips. "I suppose I'll leave a present for Stephens." He reaches down and loops the cord around my balls, cinches it tight, tight, even tighter, until I groan and jerk against the restraints. But that's only the beginning. After he's done separating my balls from my cock, he proceeds to bind each individual testicle, and then lace the cord all the way up my cock. It's mercilessly tight, and my cock is throbbing painfully even before he's done. Detective Swint stands back and admires his work, gives a satisfied nod. "Don't keep it that way too long, boy, or else you might lose it."

I groan with frustration and look up at him, pleading. That elicits and frosty chuckle. "All right," he calls to his slave. "I'm done here."

The slave opens the door. "Sir, yes Sir!"

With that, Detective Swint turns and leaves me alone, locking the door behind him.

I let out one long sigh and tug on my restraints. They're firm. I look down at my cock. It's gone purple already, the skin bulging and shiny. It throbs and aches with each heartbeat. God, it hurts! This can't be good.

I hear muffled voices outside the door. I can't tell what they're saying but I recognize Detective Swint and Officer Stephens. Finally the conversation ends and the door is unlocked. Stephens enters. He's still wearing his full uniform, Stetson, leather gloves and aviator sunglasses. He pauses a moment, stares at me on the bed, then shuts and locks the door behind him.

He approaches and I stare up into his face, see two reflections of myself there. I look so pathetic, bound and help-less, gagged with my asshole fucked raw. I grunt as loudly as I can and nod toward my cock. Stephens casts his glance there. He crosses his arms lets out a long sigh.

"I was afraid he'd do that."

I whimper.

Stephens removes his Stetson and places it upside down on the night table, puts the sunglasses and gloves inside it. He bends to inspect my bound cock, notes the end of the cord, leaves his hand there while he regards me. His eyes are hard, his jaw determined. "Listen to me, boy: quick is better than slow here. It hurts like hell but it's over fast." He searches my eyes. "Do you trust me?"

I nod without thinking. I do trust him, as crazy as that seems. I do. He presses his hand firmly against my forehead, puts his lips to my ear. I feel his hand fumble for the loose end of the cord.

"Gooooood boy. . ." he croons. "Just breathe. Gooooood boy. . ."

I inhale through the piss gag, and just then, Officer Stephens quickly pulls at the leather cord.

It feels like he's slashing at my nuts with a razor! No, a scalpel. A razor would make straight gashes, but this fire wraps around my scrotum, bisects it, spiraling up and down as it shreds my cock and nuts. I'm inhaling but suddenly the air reverses itself in my lungs and I start to scream. Jesus Fucking Christ! The sound is terrible and unreal in my ears, a gurgling moan. It scares me even though I know I'm the one making it. In the background is Officer Stephens' voice, soothing and warm. "Thaaat's okay, boy. Let it out. I'm here for you. I understand, boy. Let it out. . ."

And still there's more cord. The pain intensifies as he gets closer to the skin. I'm jerking and twisting on the bed, grateful for the restraints that hold me in place. I shut my eyes and shout through the gag, emptying myself of pain and air. "I understand, boy. I understand. Just let it out." And all of a sudden he's done -- either that, or the endorphins have just kicked in. I'm suffused with warmth, my cock free and throbbing, the cord nothing but a gossamer presence on my thigh.

"Goooood boy. Gooooood boy. You make me proud, boy."

I nod, grateful for the compliment. Sweat breaks out all over me. I relax into the restraints, melt into a pool of my own sweat.

Officer Stephens exhales and stands up. He puts his hands on his belt and looks down at me. His eyes are kind. He takes a moment to look at my cock and retrieve the leather cord, placing it on the night stand.

"Swint's a real son of a bitch, boy. I'm sorry."

Sorry? Sorry he put my ass in the pot, or sorry Swint did that to me? Something about Officer Stephens' tone, the look in his eyes, tells me that he too, sometime in the past, has suffered at the hands of Detective Swint. He knows that wrapped-cock trick from personal experience.

Stephens had worried about me. That's plain to see on his face. He unsnaps his duty belt and hangs it off the foot of the bed. He sits on the mattress and removes his boots, stands and unsnaps his police shirt. He opens it with his back to me, twists his arms free, back muscles rippling. He looks over his shoulder.

"I'm fixing to do this right, boy."

I don't know what he means, and the confusion must show on my face. Officer Stephens places the shirt on the steel bed frame, stands there a moment shirtless in his gray trousers, then strips those off as well. Finally he's left with just socks and a jock. I saw him this morning completely nude, but somehow, this is more intimate. He's removed his uniform for no other reason than to come down to my level. The socks and jock come off, and he takes a last moment to stroke my body. He removes the piss gag, tosses it dismissively over his shoulder, then holds the collar padlock in his hand and considers. He shakes his head. "This too," he says. He roots in his pants for the key and removes the chain from around my neck. I lay there stunned and compliant. He's made some kind of decision here. Rules have changed.

He kneels on the bed, reaches over my head and frees my hands from the wrist restraints. I bring them close to my heart and massage the wrists while he pays attention to my feet, removes my boots and socks and releases my ankles. I bring my knees up to my chest, fetal.

He kneels on all fours above me, strokes me tenderly, starting at my face and working down my body. Again and again, one touch after another, each feather-light and warm. His hands unknot me, relax me. My hands unclench. My legs extend. Finally I lay there utterly limp, just as helpless as before but this time without restraints. His face is close to mine. I notice new details -- laugh lines at his mouth, faint network of burst blood vessels in his cheeks, flecks of brown in his eyes. His expression is serious yet open as he continues to stroke me, with both hands now, palms flat against my body. The bloom of sweat from my endorphin rush is cooling on my skin, chilling me, but his warm hands keep the cold at bay.

And that's when it happens. Without thinking about it, with no conscious effort, I reach up and gently lay my fingers against his nipple. We both freeze, looking into each other's eyes. He looks down at my hand against his chest. My fingers are stuck there as if glued. Day pass, months. I feel his heart beat only inches away, see a faint smile creep across his lips. He caresses my hand with both of his, raises it to his lips, kisses it. I stare in amazement as Officer Stephens gently, lovingly, sucks on my fingers. My heart is beating fast now. I feel at once helpless and powerful. I bring myself up until I'm sitting, Stephens kneeling beside me, our thighs touching. I explore his chest with both hands, his gray-brown fur soft beneath my fingers, his nipples hard and rough. I bring my head close and lay it against his chest, placing my ear to the spot above his heart. I put my hands around the small of his back, and he wraps his meaty arms around me, holds me. I stay there in a cage of his smell and his warmth for several minutes, simply breathing.

He reaches behind to cradle my left buttock. He squeezes. The pressure feels so good! He lifts, and I realize that he wants me to raise myself up. I do, coming to kneel on the bed in front of him. Stephens is taller than me, but I stretch my legs slightly so that our eyes are level. He regards me, our arms entwined, and then he leans in for a kiss. I shut my eyes and give myself to him, closing the gap between us, opening my mouth. Our lips meet, his tongue entering me. I taste beer and tobacco on his breath. Does he taste piss on mine? We embrace, breathe each other's air. I nip at his ears, inhale his aftershave, his warmth bringing sweat to my skin.

He firmly grasps my shoulders and pushes me back, holds me inches away. I stare at him. What happens now? He's still in control here -- I don't doubt that for a moment. Wordlessly, gently pressuring my shoulders, he wants me to turn around. I do, going down on all fours with my back to him. I thrust my ass into the air. *Fuck me*, I think. *Please fuck me good.* Claim me all over again. But he doesn't. Instead he pulls outward on my knees, communicating by touch that I should lay face down on the bed. I do, stretching until my legs touch the cold steel frame at the far end, crossing my wrists beneath my chin. I wait there, eyes closed, while he shifts above me. He covers me, kisses my ears, hugs me protectively. I luxuriate in the sensation of his muscle and his sweat. He lifts himself up on his arms, as if doing a push-up, the muscles of his forearms knotted. He kisses me again on the back of my neck, my shoulders, my scalp, everywhere his lips can reach. Then he brings himself to his knees and begins to massage my back. I moan with pleasure -- and pain -- my muscles aching from the workouts and all this weekend's bondage. He goes deep, deeper, isolating muscles and working them both tenderly and mercilessly. I inhale, cry out.

After working my shoulders, Stephens moves down my body to the small of my back, kneading the muscles there. Every part of me hurts. I've been so worried, so mind-fucked, I haven't paid attention to my body. Now his expert hands open flood gates of stored pain more intense than any beating.

He's massaging my buttocks now, kneeling between my legs. He forces my legs outward, and as he works my glutes, his hands move closer and closer to my asshole. I feel myself flooded with pleasure radiating out from my ass. He tenderly touches and then works my sphincter, his fingers probing. I inhale, eyes shut tight, moaning. I hear him shift back there, and the next thing I know, his tongue has taken the place of his fingers. I cry out. His tongue it hot, wet, as strong as his fingers. I melt into the mattress, arms outstretched, helpless while he eats me. My cock burps pre-cum. Stephens digs in. I can feel his nose, his eyebrows, his five o'clock shadow. I'm wriggling and bucking, barely in control of myself. He comes up for air, spews a last gob of spit onto my ass, then resumes his massage. He works the back of my thighs, then strongly, strongly kneads my calves, my Achilles tendon. I'm weeping now, my face soaking the mattress.

He bends my legs back, feet in the air, and massages the toes, sucks on them. Then he rolls me over. He kneels between my legs, hot and buff and just fucking gorgeous, his fat dick at attention. He's got a serious look on his face, and he comes forward on all fours until he's looking directly into my eyes. We kiss, long and wet and wonderful, his meaty frame pressing me to the bed. He wriggles downward, traveling on his lips, kissing as he goes. He lingers at my nipples, sucking and teasing, raising gooseflesh all over my body. I cradle his head, my eyes closed in pleasure, massaging his scalp. He keeps going, kissing and biting playfully on my abs. I feel his chest fur brush my cock, and suddenly I realize what's coming. I open my eyes, prop myself up on my elbows. I feel like the back of my head is going to explode. After what I've experienced this weekend, after the beatings and the humiliation, Officer Stephens is going to suck me off.

He's got his eyes open, inspecting my cock. I can still see the lines traced there by Detective Swint's leather cord, but otherwise it feels fine. He wraps his hand around it, studies me as he gives it a gentle squeeze. I feel a sudden sharp pain, wince, but it passes quickly. I return his gaze and nod. Stephens cradles my balls in his hand, opens his mouth and slowly, carefully swallows my cock.

I shut my eyes and collapse back onto the bed, lost in his mouth. He rests on his elbows tucked beneath his chest and works my dick. Is there anything this hot man *can't* do? He twists his head while he works the shaft, up and down, his mouth a sauna while he gently squeezes my balls. My eyes are shut, my mouth open, my hands caressing his skull. I reach down, feel his broad shoulders, the strong and corded muscles of his neck. My body shudders. My breathing is ragged. I'm building toward orgasm, but Stephens wrings my nuts hard, stopping me dead in my tracks. I pull away just a bit but he's having none of it, continues to squeeze my nuts to douse the fire. I whimper and he goes back to sucking me off again, expertly, building me back toward orgasm. My breath speeds up, I rock, and once again he brings me back to earth nuts-first. I growl like a dog, and that seems to increase his passion. My cock is huge, bulging, every square inch of it super-sensitive from Swint's torture. I stare at the ceiling, gasping toward orgasm again, driven by Stephens' mouth. I suck in my breath, cover my mouth with my fist, rocking my pelvis upward.

I'm going to--

Stephens twists my nuts again.

I glare at him. He looks up at me, his mouth stuffed with my dick, still very much in control. We'll see about that. I sit up in the bed, pull myself away. The bed is small, and he's got his legs scissored around the steel footboard. I kneel, place my hands beneath his shoulders and lift. He complies, rotating himself upward, and I push back until his ass is planted at the very foot of the bed, his legs splayed out in front of him, his back vertical against the footboard. I take each of his hands and push them against the outermost verticals of the footboard, wrap the fingers there. Now I bring myself up, my head above his for the first time. I gaze into his eyes. He's stretched across the footboard as if bound, holding onto the steel, pecs stretched wide and abs heaving like bellows. His cock points toward the ceiling. I look down at him, tip his head back, consume his mouth with my own. I plant my tongue deep within, mapping out new territory between us. We breathe together for a long time as I once again taste everything Officer Stephens has to offer, then I break off and descend along his torso. His chest hair smells of pure testosterone. I lick the bony cleft between his pecs, turn my attention to each nipple, roughing them up like suspects under interrogation. Stephens inhales sharply and wriggles against the steel but keeps his hands where I put them.

That's a good boy, I think. I continue downward, licking and biting, finally landing in my familiar destination. I take Stephens' cock in my mouth and suck him for all he's worth. I've sucked him so much in the last four days I know the terrain of his cock by heart. Every square inch, every vein and dimple is familiar and dear. But now it's different. If I want to pull away, I do. If I want to take it deep, I do. If I want to tongue his piss slit, I do. Stephens moans and wriggles. I use my teeth to punctuate the blow job, paying him back for this weekend's abuses. That's for the piss milkshakes, I think, leaving a mark. That's for that asswhupping you gave me first night. That's for leaving me alone with Fischer. And THAT'S for losing my ass in that goddamned card game!

"Ah, fuck!" he cries out, glares down at me. I return the stare, note that he keeps his hands pinned right where I left them.

This man knows how to follow orders. His uniform shirt hangs from the corner of the footboard, the fabric draped over his hand. The sight of his shiny badge gets me all the harder, and I begin concentrating on blowing this officer. I work him good, sucking and throating, gently massaging his balls as I go. Now I look up and see he's got his eyes closed again, his face twisted with ecstasy. I slowly build the intensity, working toward climax. He doesn't rise as quickly as I did -- his cock hasn't been roped up the way mine was -- but I bring him up the mountain with a confidence borne of practice. I know what this man likes. And just at the moment he's about to come, just as he's gone slack against the footboard and surrendered all control to me, I pull away and let his cock just dangle there. I blow cool air on his wet dick. It twitches with each heartbeat, waiting for the mouth and tongue which I now withhold. He opens his eyes, looks down at me, pleading. I keep my expression neutral as I sit there, stroking his balls and letting his erection slowly wilt. *Not yet, my friend. We're not done here. We're not done because I say so.* I reach out, take his buttocks in my hands and pull. He inches forward, away from the footboard, and comes to lie with his back on the mattress, hands stretched overhead. I push his legs upward at the knee, keep pushing until he gets the message and lifts them high into the air. I spread his ass cheeks, sniff around his sphincter. There's not the slightest odor of shit -- this lawman keeps himself clean. I pause a moment, watching his sphincter pulse in the afternoon sun, and then I plunge my tongue deep within. His moan is loud and guttural. His ass shudders. I plant my face in his hole and suck and lick as if my life depended on it. I slurp. I massage his hole with my fingers and my tongue. Stephens moans and twists on the bed, skewered by my tongue like a pig roasting on a spit.

I plant my nose just beneath his scrotum, inhale his essence like oxygen. There's a rattling sound at the door. I glance past his cock, across the room to see the doorknob twist. Someone wants in. I keep working his asshole, keeping him aloft but waiting for the knock that will break the spell. It never comes. Whoever wants in gives up and walks away, leaving us alone again. He doesn't seem to notice.

I'm tired of his ass. I push my way up his body. I briefly take his dick in my mouth again, recharge it, then move up past his abs and pecs. I carefully nuzzle his cheeks, his ears, alert for any sign of disgust on his part that I've just licked his ass. There is none. Maybe he's just a bit of a pig, since he doesn't flinch as I get closer to his lips, and when I plunge in for a deep, passionate kiss, he responds with his own eager tongue. I support myself on all fours above him, our bodies locked at lips and legs. He reaches up and strokes my chest, pinches my nipples, reaches back and swats my ass. I grunt, move my ass to show how much I like it. His hands braille their way to my hole, his fingers probing, penetrating, all the while our kiss continues. I'm moaning into his mouth now, tasting excitement on his tongue. He breaks the kiss, wriggles down the bed to give himself better access to my hole. My dick is rock hard: I feel his forearms brush it as he works my hole with more and more vigor. I'm still on all-fours, head down and staring at the mattress, mouth open. Stephens finds my nipple with his mouth, captures it between his teeth, licks. I suck in a quick breath, driven mad now, his fingers deeper and deeper in my ass.

"Please fuck me," I say. I don't know if he can hear me. I can barely hear myself. "Please fuck my ass."

He releases my nipple, gives it a final kiss, and then squirms out from beneath me. I stay in position on my hands and knees, waiting, for I know what's coming now and I really, really want it. Once he's behind me, he shifts to face my ass. I feel his pubes lightly brush my cheeks. I lean back just a bit, feel the fat head of his erect cock kiss my hole.

Stephens reaches forward to the police shirt hanging

off the footboard. He takes a tube of Vaseline from the breast pocket, holds it lengthwise along my crack, pushes a gob of lube deep into my hole. I moan again, drop my face to the mattress and push my ass high into the air. Deeper he goes. Three finger? Four? I don't know. I've been fucked so many times this weekend but now, with the flushed and bloody final rays of sunlight flooding the room, I shiver like it's my first time.

He reaches forward again, back to the breast pocket to pull out a condom. I reach up to stop his hand, hold it gently. I turn back to face him.

"No," I say. "I want you inside me. I want you to cum inside me."

Where did that come from? I've never wanted that in my life, but now I do. I want him to fill me with his cum, give me something of himself that I can hold inside forever. Stephens shakes his head, gently, and breaks my grip with a firmness that leaves no room for debate. I turn my eyes back to the mattress.

I hear him open the condom package, feel the bed shift as he pulls it on. A moment later the head of his cock is pressing against my sphincter. Stephens widens my hole with his thumbs, and then slowly, lovingly, pushes himself into my gut. I let out a long, satisfied moan. I'm right where I belong, and so is he. His movements are slow. He knows what he's doing. Out and back. Out and back. His cock fills every fold of my ass, exciting nerves I didn't know I had, nerves that have waited there since birth for just the right man to come along. Heat spreads from my ass like alcohol, like magic bubbling deep from within. Faster now, the creaking of the bed telling me that Officer Stephens is settling in. I rock with him, aware of truncated shouts in the room. He reaches forward, grabs my shoulders and pulls himself in. He drives my legs apart like a wedge, compressing my spine. I buck my head into the air and make more noise, animal grunts. Stephens roars as well, masculine and passionate.

We float, drifting on a glassy sea of sweat and cum. The bed frame squeals. The world turns inside out. The very air is frozen in time. Our fucking is the engine that powers the universe. I'm aware of noises outside. The party is breaking up, masters leaving with their slaves. Car doors slam. Motorcycles fire to life. None of it matters because Stephens is filling me with his cock, slapping his balls against my ass. I reach back to stroke my penis, but stop immediately when the lightning flash across my eyes announces I'm about to cum. I don't want to bring us crashing down a moment too soon. Stephens pulls out, lifts upward on my shoulders. "Get back here, boy," he says, his breath ragged. I come up on my knees and look over my shoulder. Stephens is standing by the side of the bed now, and he pushes me backward. I topple onto my back, my head at the head of the bed, and he kneels between my legs and lifts them into the air. I've only a second to register him, pecs and abs shining with sweat, chest heaving, face intent, as he plunges his stiff cock back into my ass.

"Ahhhh, yes!" I shout.

Stephens is quiet, intent on his work. He nails my ass like a pile-driver, powerful and single-minded. My head is close to the headboard, each thrust conducted up my body, threatening to bash me against the steel. I brace myself, driving my ass deeper onto his cock. He's pounding away, head tilted upward, sweat dripping from his brow. I can't stand it any longer -- I reach down stroke my cock. The feeling sends a shiver through me, an electric current that clenches my asshole tightly around him. He moans. I suddenly become aware of my approaching orgasm, see it in my mind as a wave rushing toward me. I could no more hold it back than I could hold back the sea. There's a quiver in Stephens' hips now, no doubt his own wave threatening to break.

I'm determined to live in this moment forever, to burn every detail into memory. Stephens kneels between my raised legs, muscled torso slick with sweat, skin set afire by the final rays of the sun. His chin is inclined upward, his eyes half closed, arms spread wide as he tightly grasps my ankles. Behind him on the bed frame hangs his police shirt and duty belt, badge glinting just over his shoulder. His pelvis is a blur of motion as he fucks me, driving his fat cock into my asshole again and again and again. And again. And again!

AND AGAIN!

BANG! We blow ourselves out of the room.

He shouts something, screams it, face twisted toward the ceiling. His hands squeeze my ankles nearly hard enough to pop the joints. My cock erupts a fountain of jizz, and in some weird trick of time I see a ropy globule of it rotating in the space above our bed, end over end over end like a computer graphic trick, before finally it splatters against my chest. The whole bed shudders, the whole goddamned room. And in another moment of bliss, we both come back to ourselves. Back to earth. Back to sweat and stink and the stained mattress and the sounds of men moving around outside.

We stay that way for several moments, breathing deeply, recovering. Tension drains from his shoulders. His arms relax. He lowers my ankles to the bed, his cock sliding free of my asshole. He looks at me, eyes unreadable, chest heaving. I nod, feeling the same thing, whatever it is. He rubs my thighs, massages them. I reach up and stroke his nipples. His cock is softening. He reaches down and pulls the condom from it, leans to the side of the bed for the wastebasket. I reach up to stop his hand and he looks at me, question in his eyes. I take the condom, upend it above my chest and pour his juice out onto me. Stephens smiles, reaches down and slides his hand along my chest and abs, up and down, mixing our jizz together. Then he leans forward, wraps his arms around me. His head on my shoulder, he relaxes and I support him. Warm and wet, covered in perspiration, the room smelling of cum. I doze.

A knock on the door starts us both. Stephens inhales, lifts his head. I'm a bit confused, not sure the knock was real. Then it comes again, followed by Fischer's voice through the door.

"Hey, bud. We got work to do out here." He sounds. . . tentative? Sympathetic? Stephens turns back toward the door. "Yeah, I'm coming." He exhales a long and heavy sigh.

I look up at him. "Do you need me out there?" I pause, uncertain. "Sir?"

He looks at me a bit confused, then shakes his head. "No. You'll be needed later to clean up." He leans down then and kisses me, long and deep, then lifts himself up. Our bodies don't want to let go, the skin of our chests and stomachs fused together. He dresses quickly and silently, stands beside the bed in the darkened room, once again in full uniform. He looks down at me. Something has changed between us, that overlay of fear gone. It's replaced by something more nourishing.

Admiration? Comfort?

Love?

God help me.

It's just fatigue -- hunger and fatigue and the glow from a really, really good fuck. Sure. That's all it is. He turns toward the door but glances back as if he's forgotten something. He looks around the room, considers and removes handcuffs from his duty belt. "Put your hands up through the headrest there, boy." I glance upward at the head rest and obey. He leans over and cuffs my wrists, securing me to the bed. He smiles. "That should keep you out of trouble."

"Yes, Sir."

He leans over for a final kiss, and then he's gone, locking the door behind him.

I doze for a while, still warm in the glow. My head spins as I come down, lost in too many thoughts. What happened between us was genuine. If not love, then affection. He only needed me for this party today, but he can't mean to harm me now. Not after what just happened.

But, logically, how can he afford to let me go? What about Fischer? If he needs to get rid of me -- and that must be going through his mind -- then Fischer could do the dirty work. Would Stephens allow that?

Despite the fact that I'm laying hand-cuffed to his bed, covered in the remainder of his cum, it seems so unreal. Nothing I can do now. Later. Later there will be time to think. But my relationship to Stephens isn't the only thing that's different. I'm different. I've endured abuse this weekend far worse than anything I ever thought possible, shattered through every limit. There's a strength inside me I didn't know I had. And to balance the pain has been ecstasy powerful enough drive a turbine. Whatever happens, I'm going to get through the next several hours. Life for me will forever be more vivid, more real. More car doors outside, boots on gravel. There's no clock visible in here but it must be getting late. I hear voices out there, Fischer and Stephens saying goodbye to the guests. I can't make out exactly what's being said over the engine noise. One by one the other voices

leave until it's only the two of them, walking slowly. I can only hear the occasional word: ". .
. never. . . Fuckhole. . . mess. . ."

They're deciding what to do with me. I look up at my hands cuffed through the bed frame. Is there a way I can get free? They're moving closer to the window outside. "Ah, hell," Stephens says.

"What?"

"I got a message. My phone must have downloaded it when I went on duty last night."

"Fuckin' deadzone out here," Fischer says.

The handcuffs are solid. There's no way I'm getting out of them. I feel around the bed frame, looking for seams or screws. The sunlight is gone: it's too dark in here for me to see anything and I have to do everything by touch. These beds are cheap. They've got to disassemble somehow. If I can just figure out how, maybe I can get free. Stephens and Fischer have gone silent outside, presumably while Stephens listens to his voice mail. I hear a phone snap shut. "Son of a bitch!" he hisses.

"What?"

"Shit! I don't fuckin' believe this!"

"What?! What is it?"

Silence for a moment. I freeze. Have they heard the cuffs rattling against the bed frame? They're practically right outside the window now.

"Shit! Shit, shit, shit, shit, shit!"

"Well do you want to let me in on it or not?"

"That message," Stephens says, "was from the client."

"Huh?"

"He left it Thursday morning. Said he had a sudden business trip and couldn't make the rendezvous. He was hoping to reschedule. Shit!"

"What the hell are you talking about?" Fischer asks. "The client's been here all weekend." "Damn it, Fischer, get it through your thick redneck skull!

Whoever that is in there, it ain't the--"

He falls silent, realizing, no doubt, that I'm just on the other side of the window. Suddenly there's the crunching sound of boots on gravel as they move away. I lay there, dumbstruck. What the hell? I'm not who they think I am, but then, I thought they picked me up at random.

They must not have. They were expecting someone, someone else, and they ended up with me.

The pieces fall together. If they were expecting someone, then that means this all was pre-arranged. Someone had wanted to be stopped by the roadside, kidnapped by two cops, fucked and used for a weekend. Someone had paid for the privilege by the sound of it. But then he didn't show up at the appointed time.

And I came driving along.

I hear the front door shut now, boots in the hallway.

They're coming this way. My brain keeps making connections. Fischer and Stephens are real cops. The cruiser, the gear, the attitude -- I can't believe anyone could fake all that. And they're part of some SM group. There are scores of witnesses who saw me with them.

I hear a key inserted in the lock.

What happens now? As far as they know, they've just kidnapped some random stranger and raped him for four days. That's true as far as it goes, but I've enjoyed this weekend. This has been the hottest, most intense experience of my life.

They're not kidnappers and rapists. They thought this had all been consensual.

But now they know otherwise.

The door opens.

I lick my lips. I need more time. HOW DO I PLAY THIS?!

Stephens and Fischer spill into the room one behind the other, light flooding in from the hallway. Whatever they had planned to say it seems to go right out of their heads. Our eyes lock. The three of us stay that way for several seconds. We know. We all know.

"I heard!" I blurt out.

They glance at one another.

"I heard," I say again, "and I won't tell! This has been the hottest weekend of my life! You two are great tops and I've had a great time and I understand I'm not who you think I am but that's fine and all I want is my clothes and to get out of here!" Their stances change. They slump within their uniforms.

But Fischer recovers, jabs a gloved finger at me. "Shut your mouth, boy. I didn't give you permission to--"

He stops when Stephens slaps him on the shoulder.

"Give it a rest, bud," Stephens says.

Fischer stands there, his mouth working soundlessly. Finally, he skulks across the room and sits down on his bed, head in his hands.

Sighing, Stephens reaches into his pocket for the keys to the handcuffs.

It's the middle of the night and I'm stretched out atop the bedspread in a chain hotel. I'm fully clothed. The TV is on in front of me with the sound turned off. I can hear the occasional truck rumble by on the interstate outside the window, but otherwise it's quiet. My bags sit by the door, where I dropped them several hours ago. When I stumbled into the hotel room, I emptied my pockets and collapsed onto the bedspread. I fell asleep almost immediately but woke up just a bit ago. Now I can't get back to sleep. My brain is too busy.

After Officer Stephens freed me from the handcuffs, the spell of the previous four days had been broken. No one knew what to say or how it should be said. They asked me if I wanted to shower. I told them no, that all I wanted was some clothes. Fischer disappeared outside, came back in a few minutes later with one of my bags. I dressed. It felt strange to be wearing my clothes again, almost like a different kind of bondage, but I was thankful for them.

We agreed to get food. Fischer and Stephens changed into street clothes and we piled into their cruiser, no handcuffs for me this time. My car was parked just off the road about a half mile away. I transferred to it and then followed them for what seemed like hours to a steakhouse. I ordered enough food for two men but barely made a dent in it. I picked over the remainder while we talked.

They're real state troopers, though they're not stationed nearby. The SM club owns the ranch. They're not really married -- their absent client had a thing for married men, so that was part of the script. In fact, every aspect of my weekend had been arranged ahead of time: the piss shakes, the bondage, the cigars -- everything. That it meshed so well with my own fetishes was an accident. I suppose I should count myself lucky the guy wasn't into shit or blood. Stephens and Fischer had gotten the idea to offer up fantasy weekends. It was risky, of course, since they were using real equipment, but they had been careful. Or so they thought. Their client had been vetted beforehand, everything mapped out and safeguards put in place. "The only thing we didn't count on," Fischer said, "was you driving along instead of him." I sat there and nibbled, my stomach about to burst. I wanted to get angry but I just couldn't. I told them that almost everything they did to me was great. The only thing I hadn't liked was thinking they would kill me. They looked at each other then, their discomfort painful to watch. After dinner they led me to this hotel. In the parking lot outside, Stephens helped me with my bags while Fischer stayed in the cruiser. I didn't know what to say. Neither did he.

Before I headed into the lobby, he looked around to make sure no one was watching, then wrapped his arms around me and kissed me long and hard. And it was the same magic all over again. I didn't need to be tied up. I didn't need to fear for my life. I was in the arms of an incredible man and that was more than enough. It wasn't until I got into the room that I found the restaurant napkin he had stuffed into my back pocket.

Now it's the middle of the night I'm hungry again. I should go find an all-night diner. I tried to jerk off but it was useless. My dick has put out a Do Not Disturb sign and I can't say I blame it. So I'm just laying here, watching some celebrity train wreck play out silently on the TV.

I went to the toilet after I woke up, and when I dropped my pants I caught a glimpse of my ass in the mirror. There was writing there, small black capitals, and after some confusion I remembered Stephens doing that while I was up in the sling. I struggled for several moments to read the message, backwards and upside down. Finally I got it:

PROPERTY OF OFFICER STEPHENS

I've never believed in fate or any of that mystical bullshit. But staring at my ass in the mirror, alone in the dead of night, his scent thick on my skin and his image in my memory, I found it hard to deny.

Christ, enough of this! There's plenty of time later to sort out what it all means. Right now I need food and rest, and tomorrow I need to get home, return to my life, to myself.

On the table by the door is the steakhouse napkin. Written in blue ink on that napkin is an e-mail address.

And Texas will always be here.